### JEFF ELLIOTT

# MEDITERRANEAN CRUISE 1984

## TIMEKEEPERS PLAN FOR THE PARABELLUM TERRORIST

iUniverse

**MEDITERRANEAN CRUISE 1984**
**TIMEKEEPERS PLAN FOR THE PARABELLUM TERRORIST**

Copyright © 2017 Jeff Elliott.

All rights reserved. No part of this book may be used or reproduced by any means, graphic, electronic, or mechanical, including photocopying, recording, taping or by any information storage retrieval system without the written permission of the author except in the case of brief quotations embodied in critical articles and reviews.

This is a work of fiction. All of the characters, names, incidents, organizations, and dialogue in this novel are either the products of the author's imagination or are used fictitiously.

iUniverse books may be ordered through booksellers or by contacting:

iUniverse
1663 Liberty Drive
Bloomington, IN 47403
www.iuniverse.com
1-800-Authors (1-800-288-4677)

Because of the dynamic nature of the Internet, any web addresses or links contained in this book may have changed since publication and may no longer be valid. The views expressed in this work are solely those of the author and do not necessarily reflect the views of the publisher, and the publisher hereby disclaims any responsibility for them.

Any people depicted in stock imagery provided by Thinkstock are models, and such images are being used for illustrative purposes only. Certain stock imagery © Thinkstock.

ISBN: 978-1-5320-1401-7 (sc)
ISBN: 978-1-5320-1397-3 (e)

Library of Congress Control Number: 2017902316

Print information available on the last page.

iUniverse rev. date: 03/03/2017

# DEDICATION

This book is dedicated to the memory of my best buddy and fellow Swift Boat Gunner in Vietnam, Glen Cameron (Cam) Keene. He was a good man and better friend. He loved hunting, fishing, and marine biology; most of, all his family. Cam was proud to be an Alabama son.

Born on the 4th of July 1946, and killed in action, the 2nd of July 1969 by a mortar explosion; buried in his beloved Fairhope, Alabama. American Patriot and Hero

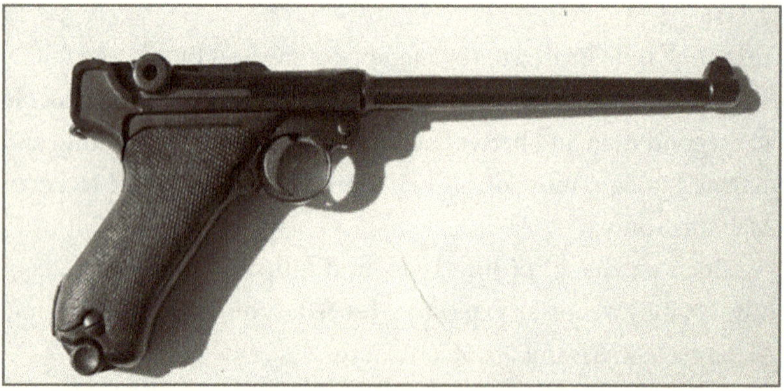

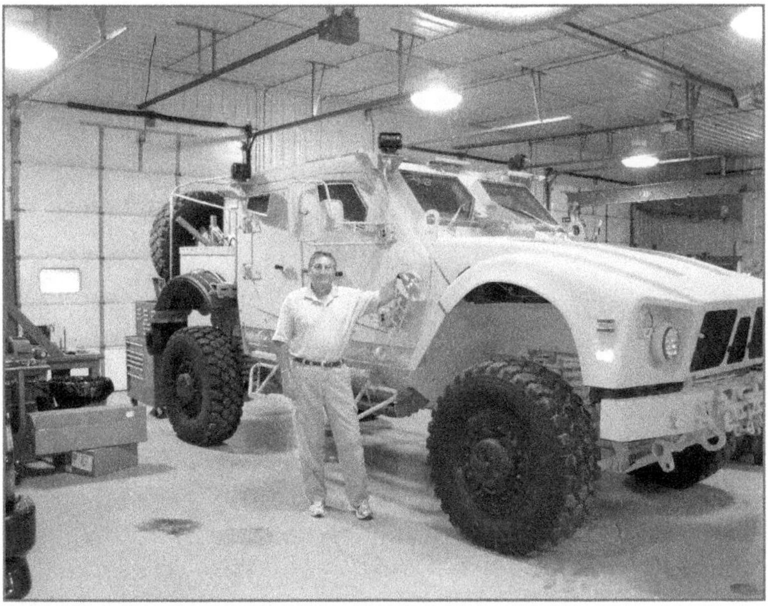

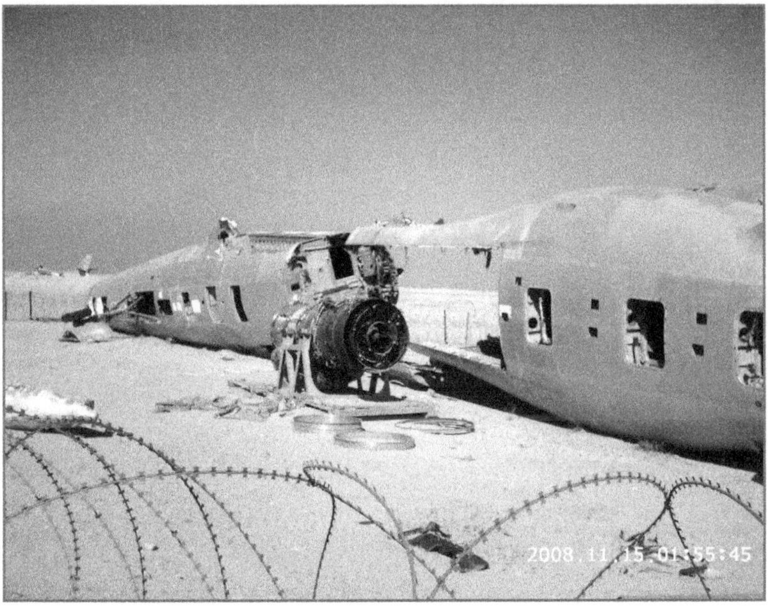
2008.11.15.01:55:45

# CHAPTER 1

**SUNDAY MARCH 3, 1984.** The morning was cool, and a light fog was hugging the low country of South Carolina. In the northern sky a DC-10 made its approach into the Charleston International Airport. To those who noticed, it appeared to be suspended by an invisible string. The huge plane hung lazily in the heaven. On board was a full complement of crew and passengers, one particular individual was Philip Mattingly, a Senior Chief Gunner's Mate in the US Navy. Mattingly was transferring from San Diego, California to Charleston, South Carolina. He had completed his tour of shore duty, and now it was time to return to sea. Mattingly was assigned, as an instructor, to the Fleet gun school located on the Naval Station, at 32$^{nd}$ Street.

He was on his way to his new assignment, duty aboard the USS Mount Mitchell, AE 53. The Mount Mitchell, the first ammunition ship of its class, designed to steam anywhere in the world that US Navy combat ships may be sent, or be called to action. The Mount Mitchell's mission was not that of a primary combatant nature, but one of providing the steady flow of ordinance, any type, any time, and delivered pretty-much on demand; keeping the fleet rearmed anywhere in the theater of operation. Her three Foster Wheeler boilers could push her through the water at 20 knots. The ship's capabilities made her a vital link in the logistic chain of freedom.

Senior Chief Mattingly had researched his ship while in San Diego. He studied any information he could find, especially the equipment and upcoming schedule. He knew the ship was equipped with four 3" 50 caliber dual purpose twin gun mounts. Two mounts located on the bow, and two aft, forward of the helicopter landing deck...simply known as the "helo deck". His new job also included managing the ammunition on board, and leading the crew that maintain these items. Many individuals were involved in this task, and he did not take his responsibilities lightly. The guns were installed for the express purpose of self-defense. The overwhelming majority of the ordnance on board was for fleet issue, this included *special weapons*.

Phillip only two weeks earlier, had completed the ammunition management course in San Diego, and had spent 10 days visiting with his 15-year-old daughter. He and his ex-wife Susan had divorced eight years before, but were still remarkably close friends, and took their parenting duties seriously. Susan had moved on in her relationship with an engineer she met in the shipyard while doing consulting work for the insurance company where she worked.

Phillip's thoughts turned to Susan. He was remembering their last discussion. The topic of remarriage was broached by him. It was at that moment he learned of her new friend. The divorce had been civil, but the memories still remained. Constant family separation due to back-to-back deployments, haunting memories of Vietnam, and an overbearing mother-in-law had been their downfall.

Suddenly the bounce of the DC 10 landing on the concrete runway, and the abrupt reversal of the engine thrusters, brought him back to the present. As the mammoth jet slowed, Philip peered out the window. He observed signs of new construction in the area. The airport had been upgraded. The Charleston International Airport was now in service. He had leaned forward slightly to scan the surroundings and noticed several military aircraft, C-141, C-17 and C-5 cargo jets far across the tarmac still parked precisely and neatly in military fashion, in a row. He was thinking to himself. How easy for an enemy agent to make one strike, and render all these aircraft out of commission. The man seated next to him spoke and startled him out of his thought.

"The Air Force and the city of Charleston share the facility here." Phil looked at the man raised his eyebrows in a silent understanding gesture. He turned and continued looking out of the window at the runway, and surrounding buildings until the plane came to a stop at the terminal. Once again his thoughts turned to Susan. Their distance was increasing in more than just the geographical sense.

Philip was completing the walk from one end of the terminal, where he had deplaned, to the extreme opposite end of Concourse A where the baggage claim area is located, when he heard a voice.

"It seems as if they go out of their way to park the airplane as far away from the baggage areas as possible, don't it?" Phil looked up to recognize a familiar face. It was the man who sat next to him on the flight. "Yeah," Phil answered, "I'm glad this isn't LAX", referring to the sprawl of Los Angeles International Airport in California. They each smiled and chuckled lightly. Then the man said, "Good luck Chief". Phil raised his hand in sort of a half salute and a smile. "Thanks, the same to you."

He retrieved his duffel from the baggage carrousel, and headed for the exit. As he stepped onto the sidewalk, a taxi stopped in front of him. The short redheaded woman driver about 60 jumped out, "How about a ride sailor?" He was momentarily caught off guard.

"Sure beautiful." he replied.

The lady driver laughed. "Ain't had anybody call me beautiful since last night. I hauled three drunks back to a merchant ship docked at the Navy base. You ain't drunk are you there sailor?"

Both laughed simultaneously while loading his bag into the trunk of the taxi. "No; not for a long time now." He responded while sliding into the rear seat. He studied her as the slightly rounded woman moved quickly to the driver side and squeezed in behind the wheel. The driver asked, "Where to cutie?"

Phil glanced into the rearview mirror; the alert eyes of the driver were locked on his. "Navy base please, USS Mount Mitchell."

"Be there in a jiff," she stated. "Say, is that's the ship women recently got assigned on board?"

Phil's eyes moved to the license attached to the visor by three heat-cracked, half melted rubber bands. "Sure is Darlene. Want to come along and sign on?"

Her eyes pass by the license. "Not a good likeness; looks more like a mug shot. No, I'z married to a Navy man for twenty seven years. Husband was a boatswain mate."

"Was?" Phil questioned.

"Yeah he sailed off one day never came back."

"I'm sorry to hear that Darlene."

"Don't make any difference; he was a miserable son of a bitch. He still sends me 900 bucks a month anyway; says he feels obligated since we were hitched for so long, and still are. He retired four years ago; runs a fishing boat out of Morehead city, maybe someday...," She paused.

Phil turned his head towards the window with thoughts of Susan. "Yeah, I know what you mean," he whispered.

All was quiet as the taxi approached the main gate of the Naval Station. The cab rolled to a stop, and a well-built black man dressed in a freshly pressed police uniform approach the window where Phil was sitting.

"ID, please sir." Phil handed his Navy ID card to the officer.

After careful examination of the card he handed it back and said, "Have a good day Senior Chief."

Phil smiled and responded with, "You as well sir." The taxi rolled on through the gate, made a right turn and headed towards pier 'N' or November as the Navy calls it, in accordance with the phonetic alphabet.

"Here we are lover; this is as far as I can go, regulations you know." Phil's thoughts turned to his dad as he reached for his money clip. His father had given him the money clip on his 21$^{st}$ birthday. He pulled off three fives, and handed it to Darlene.

"Your change is..." she muttered.

Phil offered, "Please keep it; let me buy you a coffee." Darlene acknowledged and said, "Thanks handsome, I'll return the favor some time." They both knew they would most likely never cross paths again.

Phil watched as the taxi pulled away. Darlene smiled and waved a friendly gesture. Phil waved and smiled in return.

While entering through the security gate at the head of the pier, his thoughts instantly returned to the airport, and the baggage claim area. There it was, the USS Mt Mitchell.

"Yep, Wouldn't have it any other way, son-of-a...," The ship was all the way at the end of the pier, located at the stern was the 50 foot brow which looked to be at about a 45° angle leading up to the quarterdeck. He began the long walk down the pier, with his bag hoisted on his shoulder.

As he reached the foot of the brow, the messenger of the watch (MOOW) hurried down the steep incline to give Phil a hand.

"Can I give you a hand there senior?" The young seaman asked, "That's a long walk down the pier, and this is a steep climb when the tide is in."

"Yes," as he took a breath for the second part of his reply, "I would appreciate that very much." Upon reaching the quarterdeck

Phil saluted the national ensign flying on the fantail, and turned to salute the officer of the deck.

"Senior Chief Petty Officer Mattingly, reporting on board for duty sir." The officer of the deck returned the salute and replied, "Welcome aboard shipmate."

Phil handed over his packet of orders, and was officially recorded into the ship's quarterdeck log by the Petty Officer of The Watch, (POOW).

"Can't do much checking in today", said the OOD, "since today is Sunday, only the duty section is on board. But we can get you checked in, and get you a place to sleep. We'll have someone from the CPO mess come up to help you get your gear stowed, and find you a bunk and a locker."

"Sounds great, and perhaps a cup of coffee too?" "No problem," said the OOD, "the best damn coffee in the fleet is brewed right here."

"Wow! That's a mighty impressive set of ribbons you're wearing Senior, is that the Silver Star?" Phil had been awarded The Silver Star for actions during a firefight on a river in Vietnam. He didn't speak of it much.

"Yes...," he paused. Trying to shift the attention away from himself he asked, "Say, what's the mood like with females on board?" The answer came immediately.

"Very good" a female voice answered. Phil turned to see a female chief standing behind him. She smiled and extended her hand. "Chief Cornell, disbursing clerk, and you'll find we pull our share of the load around here."

Phil recovered quickly, "I'm sure, if they're all as efficient as you." Insinuating to the short time it had taken her to appear on the quarterdeck.

"I have duty this weekend, but I also live on board", she replied, "and I also know what it's like to stand around and wait, we'll have one of the mess cooks come up and get your bag."

Phil replied, "That's okay, I think I can handle it from here, I have finally caught my breath after the hike."

Chief Cornell acknowledged that fact, "Yes it is a long hike." She turned headed towards the mess, with Phil following close behind.

They entered the CPO mess; Phil took a close look around at what was to be his new home for at least the next two years. The mess room was large enough to seat about 20 people. The décor, of nautical furniture, pictures, and lamps made from old wooden block and tackle, gave the appearance of an older ship, one from a by-gone era, possibly one of, iron men and wooden ships.

Chief Cornell turned with a cup of coffee and handed it to Phil. "Gail." She said.

"Excuse me," Phil expressed.

"Linda Gail, is my name, please call me Gail, and yours?"

"Philip, Phil if you don't mind?"

"I don't mind," As she looked up with a cheerful smile and two gorgeous blue eyes. Phil felt as if he had been suddenly stricken with a severe case of stupid.

"Please excuse me; I wasn't expecting, well, a chief with your…, your qualifications." What an idiotic thing to say, assumed Phil.

Gail laughed, "Don't worry, soon you'll get used to us."

"Us?" He questioned with raised eyebrows.

"There are five more female chiefs in here," Gail replied, "and each one is as off limits as I am. We are professional women."

Phil smiled, and Chief Cornell realized what she had now said. Her smooth young face started to redden. Phil relaxed and grinned realizing she was somewhat off her game too.

"I'm sure you all are." He had detected a tenseness and embarrassment in Cornell's voice. Soon that tenseness would be gone. Gail pointed to a chart located on the bulkhead. "Number eight?"

Phil replied "Number eight?"

"Your bunk number, and there should be corresponding empty locker there too. We made room for you when we received your advanced orders. By-the-way, I am the CPO Mess Treasurer and Caterer; I take care of all the financials for the mess, and supervise the mess cooks assigned to us."

He studied the chart, "I don't see your name here."

Gail replied, "Different chart, different bunk room."

"Damn the bad luck and I was under the impression this was the new Navy."

Gail came back with, "New Navy, old problems." She smiled again extended her hand and said, "Welcome aboard Phil." He acknowledged the friendly gesture and added "Best welcome aboard I've ever had."

Gail turned and walked away, Phil continued to watch as the five foot seven blonde exited through the door. He thought to himself, beautiful, blue-eyed blonde, and single. He had detected before, her left hand had no ring, but the right one did. This wasn't merely a safety factor of not wearing jewelry on board a ship. He wondered, what exactly what her story was.

The door reopened and there was Gail. "Oh yes, brunch at 1000 hours."

Their eyes locked, "It's a date." He said. She smiled and disappeared through the doorway. Phil started dragging his seabag into the male berthing area.

As he was arranging his personal effects into the limited space he was allotted, he couldn't help thinking; this one irritation had, on a few occasions, caused him to consider retirement at his twenty year mark. Phil muttered to himself "This isn't the way a person is supposed to live, everything you own cramped into a locker six feet tall, thirty three inches wide, and eighteen inches deep." Residing on board the ship, even a modern one, was cramped at best. After managing to compact everything into his new locker, he headed for the shower. Phil had traveled most of the night to get to Charleston, and wanted to freshen up. He was about to enter the wash room, when through the door came a wet, short man clad only in shower shoes and a drooping towel.

"Sons of a bitches, they do it every damn time!" ranted the soggy chief. "Damn snipes, damn navy, dammit all and I have the next watch!" As the little wet angry man plodded off, Phil noticed; one red shower shoe, and one green one, "how strange, must be a boatswain mate," he said out loud, "who else would have shower shoes matching the running light pattern for a ship? Red for port, and green for starboard" He laughed to himself as he viewed the wet footprints disappeared around the corner.

As Phil prepared to shower, he realized exactly what had made the pudgy little man so angry. No hot water! This was often a problem on older ships, but he didn't believe this should be a problem, at least alongside the pier. The phrase "Welcome aboard shipmate," returned to his mind.

Phil took his cold shower and contemplated of the words uttered by Gail earlier, "New Navy, old problems." Apropos, he thought, those words fit the present situation to a "T". He put on his wash-khaki uniform (work uniform for officers and chiefs) and prepared to enter the mess for brunch.

By this time, three other chiefs had gathered in the mess, sitting and eating grilled ham and cheese sandwiches. Each took turns introducing their selves, and welcoming him aboard. They invited him to sit with them. The first chief to introduce himself was Chief John Bagley, electronics chief on board. Bagley said, "If you have any problems with the electronics on any of the gear, just let me know, and I'll be there to help." The second was the chief storekeeper who informed him," Senior, if you ain't got it, and you need it, I can get it."

Phil laughed and said "that's good to know, how about ordering up some hot water for the showers." The first two chiefs laughed out loud, almost cackling, as the third chief introduced himself. "I'm Chief Machinist Mate Robinson, duty engineer today."

Phil noticed Robinson's face was blushing as he started making excuses as to why there was no hot water. The machinist mates on board the ship are responsible for all the auxiliary systems which include hot water for all the showers, cooking and etc.

While everyone was enjoying a good laugh at the expense of Chief Robinson, a tall lanky female chief entered the mess. Phil's eyes immediately turned to her. She poured herself a cup of coffee and sat down at the table across from him.

"Welcome aboard shipmate, I'm Pat Allen, personnel chief."

Phil responded and was shaking hands and introducing himself, when Gail entered into the mess. She looked at Phil and then shifted her icy stare over to Pat. Philip stood up as if some high-ranking officer had walked in. He realized that he was the only one standing, and still holding Pat's hand. Gail's eyes turned back to Phil, and soften somewhat in their intensity. It was then she shifted her focus to the joined hands. Phil released the warm soft hand, in a manner not unlike a child that had been caught with his hand in the cookie jar.

Pat spoke and broke the silence. "Do you open doors too?" She was obviously by everyone present, referring to the manner in which Phil had risen from his chair when Gail entered the space.

As he eased himself back in into his chair, he said "This is going to take some getting used to. I'm not accustomed to having this sort of company in the CPO mess."

Chief Bagley stated "Hey Senior, don't spoil the young chiefs, they are just about to get use to us crusty old farts." They all chuckled lightly, but Phil could detect tension in the atmosphere.

Gail looked at Phil and reassured him, "It's nice to know that there is at least one gentleman on board anyway." There were oohs, aahs and ouches, from all the male chiefs.

Pat retorted with, "knock it off, Blondie!"

"Stuff it bitch!" came the angry reply from Gail.

Phil was quite shocked at the rapid deterioration of the conversation. In the blink of the eye, Pat was on her feet and headed for Gail. She stood her ground.

Phil came to his senses and realized what was happening raised his hand and brought it crashing down on the table rattling all the cups and plates. "That's enough!" He shouted emphatically. "I don't know what the hell you two have against each other, but this is a chief's mess, not a cathouse!"

More, oohs and aahs came from the male chiefs at the end of the table.

Pat glared at everyone, and then angrily stormed out of the mess; exiting, she power slammed the door.

Gail looked at Phil, "Cat-house?" She questioned.

Phil shrugged his shoulders. "It just came out."

Gail smiled sweetly at Phil, and in a now mellifluous voice said, "Thanks for coming to the rescue King Arthur. Male chivalry isn't dead after all." She glanced around at the other chiefs and then departed.

Phil half-heartedly returned to his now cold ham and cheese sandwich, shaking his head and thinking to himself. What in the hell have I gotten myself into?

Senior Chief Mattingly had just been partially introduced to a more serious, and deadly situation than he thought he would ever run into outside of Vietnam. He turned to the other three chiefs, his brow wrinkled quizzically.

Chief Robinson spoke "No love lost between those two."

"Do you think!" was Phil's response.

"It's known Chief Cornell was able to divert one of her female Petty Officers from the influence of the Alan gang."

"The Allen gang?" Phil asked.

"Yeah, seems as though Allen has a few of the younger girls working for her out in town, doing God knows what. No one can pin anything on her, but Gail has come closer than anyone, with female sailor she managed to keep out of that gang. Thing is, Petty Officer Emmons, will not disclose anything."

Phil now understood more about his attraction to Gail. She was a genuine, caring person, just like Susan. For the remainder of the day he walked about the ship, getting the feel of his new home, meeting more of the crew, and wondering just what this tour of duty would bring. So far, things were interesting, if not downright amusing. He must however, continue to think of his duty at hand. Ensuring everything in his charge was ready for the upcoming Mediterranean cruise, with just over two weeks remaining until departure. Tomorrow he will meet with the Commanding Officer.

# CHAPTER 2

**MONDAY 5, MARCH; REVEILLE** at 0600 and breakfast were the first items of the day. After which Phil found his way to the personnel office. Gail informed him at breakfast that, he would have to find that place by himself. The way she put it was, "that is where Madam X works". He checked in at personnel and Chief Allen had his check in packet all ready to go.

"I see you are divorced." Pat stated as she flipped through his service record. "It appears some portions are missing from your history of assignments Senior, a few evaluations too."

He knew she had gone through his record with a fine tooth comb. "Yes" he answered almost angrily, "broken service after Vietnam, took some time off to find myself." He knew that this office maintains the records for the entire ship and that if Allen wanted to know something about someone all she had to do was to dig it out of their service record.

"Well senior chief, if there's anything, anything at all I can do to help you, don't hesitate to ask". She smiled and handed him his check in sheet. "We have a unique check-in procedure here; I take care of all the chiefs and a few of the officers."

Phil read the connotation in her voice but he kept smiling and asking himself, "How does she get away with this?"

With all of his required check-ins completed except disbursing, where his pay records are maintained, and his meeting with the Commanding Officer still to do, he stepped up to the pay office door. He noticed a female first class petty officer standing in the middle of the compartment reading a message; she looked up when he stepped to the half door that all ships offices had, allowing business to be conducted at that point without intrusion into the space itself.

"Welcome aboard, you must be Senior Chief Mattingly."

Phil responded with, "The one and the same."

"I'm Carol Emmons DK1; Chief Cornell told me about you…, all good I might add."

About that time Chief Allen was passing the open door, on her way to the personnel office. "Just check him in and lay off the BS."

Phil noticed the hostility towards Carol. Petty officer Emmons hastily signed Phil's record and check-in sheet. "I'll have all this worked out for you this afternoon. Looks as if you have a month's back pay, and I'd watch who I show my money to around here." Carol added, "Some people would do anything to get a few extra dollars." She looked up, handed him back his record and up-dated check- in sheet, smiled at him, took his hand, again shook it firmly and said, "Welcome aboard Senior Chief."

Allen had walked on passed them; she stopped outside her office which was just down the passageway. Phil decided to take a chance, so he asked Allen, "What is the reason for the sour feelings between you, Gail, and Petty Officer Emmons?"

She looked up at Phil and stepped in close enough for him to feel her breast against him. She whispered, "Prosperity." She winked and turned towards her office.

Phil stood there as the shapely figure turned and entered the office. His heartbeat increased out of controlled anger, he could feel the veins in his neck pulsing. This was going to be more than he had expected. He stepped up to the half- door with his check-in sheet.

Pat turned back to the door, "All done?" she asked.

"With the exception of the CO" he answered, "that is tomorrow, had to move it out a day, the CO is busy with an engineering situation."

After he finished signing his record updates, he returned to the mess for a much needed cup of coffee.

Gail walked in behind them and asked, "Buy you a cup of mud?" Referring to the consistency of the coffee that now set in the pot.

"Sure" Phil answered.

"So, how did your check-in go with Mdm. X?"

Phil looked into the two blue eyes that seemed to draw him in like a magnet. He just stared for a few seconds.

Gail smiled and stated "Check-in Phil, check-in."

He blinked his eyes quickly to break the trance. "Tell me what you know about Chief Allen". Gail's smile turned to a frown. She thought for a moment, "Why don't you ask her if you're that interested."

Phil again was momentarily caught off guard, something that seemed to be happening a lot lately, but he noticed what he reasoned might be jealousy in her voice. "No, you don't understand, I'm not interested in her, it is what she is doing I'm interested in".

Gail looked quizzically at Phil, "Why?" She asked.

"I just want to know the truth, and who I can trust around here. I feel as if I can trust you, can't I?"

Gail's expression relaxed and softened and she felt an emotion strangely build up while she explained her fear of him being drawn in by Allen, as is seemed many of the other men aboard had. "She has three females on board the ship who will do anything for her; she has this power to attract young girls into her inner circle..., then she convinces them that she knows what's best for them. Eventually, I think they are turning tricks for her or God knows what else, but I'm not sure. I believe she hires them out as escorts and actually end up sleeping with married men extorting money from them and possibly classified information".

Phil's eyes widened, "Why hasn't she been investigated?"

Gail replied, "People are afraid to accuse someone of this behavior, and none of the females have come forward. They all have taken some oath or something. She keeps them in clothes, and money. Some of these girls have never had two nickels to rub together. They come from poorer environments, and what Mdm. X offers is prosperity to them. By the time they have a year on board they are all too deeply involved. They either get pregnant or have to leave with the guilt on them or have an abortion. Allen has them transferred. No one has ever stepped up." By this time tears of anger were forming in Gail's eyes.

Phil reached for a paper napkin and handed it to her. "So now you know."

Phil replied, "Not really, but I'm getting there." He explained how Pat had acted when he turned in his check-in sheet and asked her about the hostility between the three of them.

"She, Carol, is the one you managed to keep away from Allen isn't she?"

Gail replied, "You're observant aren't you? Lieut. JG Lewis, Disbursing Officer is, mine and Carol's division officer. He is in with us. The three of us are keeping tabs on the situation trying to get one of the girls to crack, but so far they all either don't see what's happening, don't care or are just in too deeply and afraid to speak out."

Phil placed his hand on Gail's shoulder and said, "There's four of us now shipmate." Gail looked at him with eyes that were reddened from the emotion, but still remain beautiful and said, "If you really mean that, then we're glad to have your help, but it isn't going to be easy or pleasant. People are afraid of having their careers wrecked by scandal, she could tell lies that many people would be willing to believe."

"We have our Navy and our sailors to think of chief, this is a kind of activity we don't want or need. We've got to do whatever we can to get rid of this sort of infection. I have a 15-year-old daughter that's thinking about joining the Navy, and I want her and others like her to know that it is a good outfit to be in and that they are safe in it."

"Thanks for being an understanding man; a man that cares about people".

"I believe, there are lots of men who care, there may be a few who are afraid to show it, or trust their feelings, but with enough of us, stepping up to do the right thing, more of them will fall in line."

Gail said, "You're an optimist too."

"I'm not very optimistic about that coffee you offered." Gail threw up her hands and said, "Beat me, kicked me, hurt me and make me pour coffee."

At that moment Chief Robinson walked in and noticed Gail's red eyes, and said, "I see you two are getting along fine."

Phil said, "Just talking chief stuff, want to join in?"

Gail looked at Robinson, "We are discussing the Allen situation."

"Yeah, I think one of my sailors is involved also; but she is more the type that will kick your butt, than sweet talk you." They all three looked at each other silently back and forth when Phil said, "We need a plan".

# CHAPTER 3

**AT PRECISELY 1045 PHIL** knocked on the commanding officers stateroom door. There was no response; he knocked again. This time he heard a voice approaching from his six o'clock position.

"I'm here senior, just finished a meeting with the chief engineer. We have a couple of final issues to work out prior to deployment. I'm Commander Worrell, Captain of this fine vessel." He extended his hand to Philip "Welcome aboard, come on in the stateroom and have a seat."

"Thank you Capt. and yes she seems to be a very fine vessel." Phil said.

"Yes" said the Captain "she is what we make her though." The CO continued "I have reviewed your record and it seems to me that you have a very interesting background Senior. I am confident this will be to your advantage in the next few months."

Phil, a little bit confused at this statement, proceeded with a probing response "Yes sir my experience teaching at gun school in San Diego will help in training the ordinance department I suppose?"

The CO stopped writing and looked at Phil, "Heavens no, the

crew is good, I'm talking about your CIA Intel experience." Phil holding the eye-lock with the captain responded, "That is not in my record Captain."

Then Worrell smiled, "Of course not, but I have friends at the Bureau, and in the Pentagon. In a conversation with, a certain, Admiral and Master Chief Petty Officer, your name popped up."

"Of course it did Captain," he said with a sigh; "but I'm a little bit confused as to why." "You have been on board three days, and you haven't noticed tension? Heard nothing? Spoke to no one?" The captain cocked his head a little to the left and raised his eyebrows, signaling to Mattingly that it was now his turn.

"Yes sir, I've heard plenty, but to me, seeing, is believing."

"Then keep your eyes and ears open, listen carefully to the scuttlebutt. I am sure the rumor mill will find its way quickly to the new guy on board. It's just the way it works. Keep your notes close to you but take no action. I will give you more information as needed. I just do not want to be too aggressive, too soon in the process, *watch your six*. I don't want to give away our hand." He extended his hand to Phil and said "Welcome aboard shipmate and happy hunting."

As he left the stateroom, Phil couldn't help but feel more confused than when he first entered. He thought to himself, what is really going on here, and who knows what? He knew he would have to keep his cards close to his heart, and play it safe.

# CHAPTER 4

**WITH THE CHECK-IN PROCESS** complete and all of the paperwork handed in to the personnel office, he was off to meet with his division officer, Lieut. Roger Pierce. Lt. Pierce was a Mustang officer from the fleet and was enjoying his new job.

Phil knew his job would be made easier by the experience his division officer had. The primary job of the chief is to help train the young division officers, and to help make them successful. But Lieut. Pierce was the seasoned veteran, one that had risen through the ranks, and at one time had been a chief petty officer himself, hence the title Mustang.

The next few days went by without much fanfare. All hands on board Mount Mitchell were actively preparing for the upcoming Mediterranean cruise scheduled to get underway, in just two weeks, Wednesday the 28th of March.

Philip had checked and double checked the gun system on board and had determined that all systems were on go, and ready for deployment. The gun crew maintaining mounts, he viewed as superb and well trained. The task had been made simpler by the outstanding condition the guns were already in. Phil thought this to be a godsend, as compared to some of the other older equipment that could be found throughout the fleet.

Lt. Pierce was putting together final touches on all the ammo records. This was no small job, especially after a major load adjustment just prior to deployment on an ammo ship. Both Phil and Roger had begun to work together as a team and had gained much respect for the other's professional attitudes. Phil entered the weapons office where Lt. Pierce was working. "Hello there Lt., how's it going?"

"Better here than Ashdod, Israel" he answered, "there was a terrorist attack, bombing on a civilian buss; 3 killed and 9 injured."

Phil asked "Aren't we supposed to make a port visit there?"

"Yes we are, let me see…, and May…, the 11$^{th}$. That is after Athens."

"I hope things settle down before we get there," Phil stated." We'll have a lot of sailors on busses and tours all over the place."

"Yes we will, and that could be a major problem Senior. I guess we'll cross that bridge in time."

"I will be topside checking spaces, catch you later Lt."

"Ok, gunner, later."

Phil was walking about the main deck and checking the areas for which his division was responsible. His division LPO (leading petty officer), Thomas Vincent Fitzpatrick GMG1, joined him. Both of them were confident they would be ready.

Gail approached the two of them. "Hello Senior," she said in her normal sure confident voice, "all ship-shape and ready for the cruise?"

"Yeah, just a few minor touch-ups here and there, how about you chief?" Phil asked.

"Just about as ready as can be expected," answered Gail. She continued, "just a couple of more weeks and we'll see just how ready we really are."

"Ain't that the truth!" added Fitzpatrick.

She looked at Vince and said smiling, "I hope you're taking good care of senior, he's a special person."

Vince nodded his head in agreement, but had no idea of the friendship that had developed between his senior chief, and the young female chief, but he could not help but see the look in Gail's eyes, that almost gave her away. Not to mention, how all of a sudden his senior chief was now stumbling over his words.

"Did you or have you, uh, uh, will you be… Are you going to eat on board tonight?" Phil finally managed to ask.

"I was hoping to go to a nice quiet restaurant later," She said. "But I hate to be alone, it is bad for digestion." Of course eating alone has never been known to contribute to poor digestion, but it was now Gail's turn to fumble with her words.

Vince looked back and forth and smiled at the two of them, "I'll get with you later senior. Hope dinner works out for you chief." He dismissed himself and disappeared around the corner.

Gail looked up at Phil and just stood there. She waited for a while and then uttered, "Well!" "Well what?" Phil asked.

She feigned a puzzled look on her face, and had all but asked him to take her to dinner; he had not picked up the hint at first, but started to realize her meaning. Up to this point, they had only shared meals together aboard ship, including somewhat pleasant conversation with the other chiefs, mostly about the deployment. Although Phil had wanted to ask her out on several occasions, he was not sure what her reaction would be. Now was the time, and he was wasting it. He blurted out, "Go with me."

Gail reacted with "Anywhere."

"To eat, I mean," Phil responded.

"Anywhere is fine with me" she said, "anywhere."

They had been talking, and working together now for almost two weeks, and had harbored a growing feeling of attraction to one another. This would be their first time alone together off the ship. Phil looked deeply into Gail's sparkling blue eyes and he could sense more than just a superficial friendship was spawning. Both of them were acting like school kids. They each knew they were attracted to one another, but seemed to have been avoiding this moment. The moment was upon them now, and the die was cast. A few moments of silence passed while they stood there staring at one another. Gail's heart was pounding and she could feel the rush of an accelerated feeling, almost to the point of becoming dizzy. She broke the silence, "What time do you wish to leave the ship?"

Phil locked on to the words, "leave the ship," and then fully realized what had just happened. He had asked Gail for a date and she had accepted. "How about 1830, can you be ready by then?"

"I'll be sure to be on time," Gail assured him; she then turned and walked away. She had no idea at the time, where she was going, but she knew that to stay much longer would have been unwise.

She reached for the actuating lever on the main deck passageway door, and at the same time turned her eyes back to where Phil was still standing. They both smiled, and she disappeared through the doorway.

Phil thought about what had just happened, he had just asked one of the females on board for a date. He wondered how, or if, this conflicted with the policy of fraternization. He wondered if he had made a good decision. After all, they were only going to dinner and there was no direct working relationship between them.

# CHAPTER 5

**GAIL WALKED INTO THE** CPO mess dressed in a black knee length dress that accented her shapely figure. Chief Robinson was pouring himself a cup of coffee when his eyes caught sight of her. He stopped pouring, or at least he thought he did. "Holy catfish, she does own civilian clothes… And damn fine ones at that." Chief Cornell was noted for rarely leaving the ship in the evenings, and when she did, it was usually in uniform.

"What's the special occasion chief?" asked Robinson. Gail had not time to answer when Phil came in from the male bunkroom dressed in a blue blazer and tie. Robinson looked at the two of them. He said, turning his head from side to side "My, my, my, what's happening here?"

"We're going out for a change of scenery, if you please, my good man. The lovely lady and I plan to share our company with the local inhabitants of the fair city of Charleston this evening; we shall all be better off for the experience. My lady, let us not tarry, Charleston waits." Phil extended his crooked arm to Gail. She placed her hand on his extended arm. They exited the mess in a very dignified manner. Chief Robinson had by now filled his coffee cup at least twice. His look of surprise and flabbergast, turned to pain. The hot coffee ran off of the stainless steel table, were his cup sat, and onto his shoe. He jumped back and looked at the mess he had made, "Son-of-a-b....." he stopped short, realizing it would not help, so he began to clean up his disaster.

As the door closed behind them, they turn to one another, "Very well done, my good man." Gail stated.

"That was tremendously impressive dear lady." Phil said.

They nodded their heads to each other and then broke into laughter. "Did you see the look on his face?" asked Gail. "I thought he was going to swallow his tongue." "I guess we did take him by surprise"

They proceeded to the quarterdeck crossed the brow down the gangway and on to the pier. People stopped and watched as they walked by.

"I guess we will be the talk of the town tomorrow." said Phil. Gail looked up and asked, "Does it worry you?"

"It's not for me that I'm concerned," he stated "it's for you. I don't want people assuming anything exists between us that doesn't. That is my concern, and it's only for you."

Gail assured him, "Tomorrow will bring what it may, but tonight..., you are mine. By the way, where are you taking me for dinner?"

Phil answered, "I had Hardee's, McDonald's, or possibly Burger King in mind. What do you think?"

"I think we're overdressed, but lead on."

He followed with, "Then it will have to be, 82 Queen St. my lady. Nothing less will qualify."

They drove downtown in a car that Phil had borrowed from one of his fellow chiefs on board that had duty. Gail sat quietly on her side of the car. Phil looked over at her and asked. "Is everything all right? You are awfully quiet."

Gail turned and responded "Phil, how are you and your ex doing? What I mean is I feel something very strong in me and that scares me silly."

Phil smiled with understanding and said, "There's nothing serious between us. We had talked of getting remarried, but that was a while back, things are different now."

"Different, different because…?" She stopped short.

"Because of the Navy, she wanted me to get out; I said I had too much time involved. The Navy is my career, so that pretty much did it for her. She's dating an engineer at the shipyard now and she seems happy. So that shuts the door on that issue."

Gail leaned in a little closer towards Phil's side of the car and placed a trembling light kiss on his cheek.

Phil looked at her, "First time I've ever been kissed by a fellow chief…, I like it."

"Life is full of little surprises," Gail said. "First time I've ever kissed a fellow chief."

# CHAPTER 6

**DOWNTOWN THE TRAFFIC WAS** unusually light, and they quickly found a spot to park. Gail commented on this too as they only had a 3 min. walk to the restaurant.

On the stroll to the restaurant, Gail suddenly stopped and turned towards Phil. "I'm sorry about being so forward in the car, I don't know what came over me, just impulse I suppose."

Phil looked at her and said, "I'm glad you broke the ice. I wanted to do the same thing, but I didn't know how. I was also afraid of being forward, rushing into a situation."

Each of them knew there was a special bond continuing to form between them. They entered the restaurant arm in arm. During the meal they shared stories of the past and came to know the other more intimately.

Following the sumptuous dinner, they decided to go for a walk around the historic downtown section of Charleston, Gail suggested it would aid in the digestion and enjoyment of the fine meal they had just enjoyed.

"Again with the digestion." Phil chuckled. He paid the check and the two left the restaurant arm in arm.

Reaching a point at the end of the Battery, they paused and leaned against the seawall railing.

Gail pointed across the harbor, "See that light in the distance? That's Fort Sumter, and over there to the right is where Fort Johnson once stood; nothing but a sign there now. Fort Johnson is where the first shot was fired from into Fort Sumter and the Union troops at the outset of the Civil War."

"Excuse me ma'am, but that was no civil war, it was the *War Between the States*, or better known as the *War of Northern Aggression*, or *The Recent Unpleasantness*." Phil had conjured up his best southern accent, which was somewhat unusual for a native born Californian.

Gail retorted, "Begging your pardon Gen. Beauregard, I shall not make that mistake again. This is what is known as White Point Garden, and if you know your history, you know that the notorious pirate Steed Bonnet and 29 of his crew were hanged and buried here in 1718.

"You are an impressive lady." He noted. Again they were laughing and holding each other's hands and by this time giving each other reassuring hugs. The laughing subsided. All was quiet but for the gentle lapping of the Charleston Harbor waves against the seawall. They embraced in each other's arms, melting deeply into the other's eyes; slowly they move closer, their lips met.

They relaxed into each other, all nervous tension present before, was now gone. The long and passionate kiss, accented by the caressing of the gentle warm sea breeze blowing across the harbor, only enrich the flavor of this magical moment. The kiss slowly parted; but not until attracting the attention of several passersby. Gail turned her head aside and laid her cheek on Phil's warm breast.

She asked, "Is this real, am I really feeling this way inside? I've never experienced such a strong feeling. It alarms me Phil, please hold me closer."

He tightened his arms around her, as he slid his hand up her back and behind her head. "It's okay, it's okay" Phil said. "It is real."

Gail could feel his heart pounding as if it was going to run away, and then she knew that she had quite an effect on him as well.

"We had better go," Phil suggested, "This night air has the potential to make a rational person act irrational."

Gail hugged Phil tightly "Okay King Arthur, don't trust yourself?"

Phil answered, "My Queen, with you this near to me, it would be irrational to be rational, and therein lies the danger."

On the drive back to the base, Gail had snuggled under Phil's outstretched arm. She was feeling like a schoolgirl on her first date. They entered the base, parked the borrowed car, and walked down the pier towards the ship. They were keeping a distance of about 2 feet between them so as not to draw unnecessary attention. This was a tough task for both of them, considering what had taken place just a few minutes earlier. As they reached the quarterdeck each in turn presented their identification to the Officer of the Deck (OOD), and requested permission to come on board. The OOD granted permission and they strolled off towards the CPO quarters.

As they reached the mess, Gail turned around and said, "Phil, I had a wonderful time with you tonight, and I hope we can do this again sometime."

Phil said, "I wish I could afford to take you out every night, I really enjoy being with you."

Entering the mess, they were greeted by the stares and smiles along with a few raised eyebrows.

Gail, without a word, proceeded on to the female berthing area.

Phil turned towards the male bunkroom; he was about to enter when Pat Allen, whom Phil hadn't seen, spoke up.

"Well Senior, looks like you're already for the cruise." He glared at her, realizing the innuendo in her statement. He just ignored her, feeling that any comment would only legitimize this in her mind, certainly not warranted in this situation. Phil continued through the door and turned in for the night.

The thoughts of Gail raced through his head. Was this happening to him? He touched the spot on his cheek where she first kissed him, and slowly drifted off to sleep.

# CHAPTER 7

**MONDAY MORNING, REVEILLE WENT** at 0600. Everyone rolled out and prepared for a new week. This week however, was somewhat different. The Mount Mitchell would be departing on a nine month cruise Wednesday morning. Last-minute details were now being addressed to ensure sailing on time.

Phil entered the mess about 0630 and was about to start eating breakfast when Pat sat down next to him. "Good Morning Phil."

He nodded his head in return, "Morning."

"I just wanted to apologize for my comment last night. I really didn't mean it to sound as harsh and presumptuous as it came out. Several of the Chiefs got in my case, and well, I'm sorry ok?"

Phil looked at her for a moment and thought, there may be some sincerity in that statement, he was not totally convinced. "Apology accepted." He acknowledged.

Pat added, "Maybe if I'm a good girl I'll be getting an invite to dinner as well."

Phil smiled and thought to himself, not much chance of that. She stuck out her hand, "friends?" She asked.

Phil hesitantly accepted her handshake and said "yeah, sure." They smiled, dropped the handshaking and she exited the mess.

Chief Robinson spoke up, "Looks as if you're going to have your hands full Senior. They are two tough women, each in her-own right."

Phil responded, "I'll have you know chief, I make my own decisions, and I have for quite some time."

"Easy does it senior, I meant no harm, it's just everyone is talking about how Chief Cornell has her hat cocked for you, and Allen there, is a mite jealous of the way you and Cornell get along; especially dinner last night. It wouldn't surprise me if Allen didn't ask you out for dinner."

Phil looked at Robinson "You seem to know quite a lot about what goes on around here, what more do you know about Allen?"

"She is trouble with a capital T. From what I've found out since our last discussion, through the grapevine mind you, she was at the center of the controversy that ended in two divorces last year. Two shore duty types were seeing her. They got caught. She claimed she didn't know they were married, but everyone knows that was a lie. Yup, she's trouble."

"What about on board here," Phil asked. "What more have you found out about her activities?"

"She's a good personnelman, and that's all I know," was Robinson's response. Phil noticed a change in Robinson's voice, "Excuse me senior, I have some business to attend to, got to go, I'll, catch you later."

Phil watched Robinson as he left the mess. He wondered how much more Robinson knew than he had offered to tell. He finished his breakfast and then joined his division for morning quarters.

Phil was there to observe the daily muster and make sure the POD (Plan of the Day) was covered with the division, and help assign work assignments for the day. Lt Pierce would join with his division after Officers Call (the morning meeting of department heads and division officers, with the Executive Officer). Lt. Pierce would deliver any further information to the crew. The next two days were pretty much normal daily routine with all hands continuing to prep for deployment.

Wednesday morning came and departure time was set for 10hundred hours (10am). The Commanding Officer had extended liberty hours for the crew to give them time to say their goodbyes that would have to last for the next nine months. It also allowed them to take care of any last-minute occurrences that may arise.

Phil was standing on 01 level in his *Dress White* uniform, watching the 11th hour stragglers come aboard the ship. Gail, also dressed in her *Dress White* uniform, came and stood beside him at the rail.

He looked into her smiling eyes and said, "No matter how much time people have to prepare for a cruise, they all insist on waiting until the very last moment, to bring their gear on board." He pointed to several sailors coming down the pier struggling with sea bags full of clothes and other personal items. "Guitars, golf clubs, tennis rackets, bowling balls and boom boxes, what are we doing, going on a cruise or a vacation?" Phil questioned.

Wives, husbands, boyfriends, girlfriends along with a great number of children were standing on the pier waiting, crying, and saying goodbyes. Goodbyes that would have to last until next November.

This was a highly emotional time for all involved. One of the difficulties that made Navy life tough for families was the long separations these deployments required.

Deployments are expected, because that's what the Navy is all about. Everyone who joins knows this, but it doesn't seem to make it any easier.

Gail put her hand on Phil's shoulder, "It's easier for us, we live here, and we don't have anyone to leave behind, or watch sail away. This is where the adventure begins for us."

Phil chuckled a little "Yeah, I'm looking forward to the travel, Barcelona, Palma, Istanbul, Athens,-Ashdod and good old Naples, 'See Naples and Die' is the saying I believe. Sounds like a travel agent/Navy recruiter. See the exotic Mediterranean, come sail with me just sign your name here, and bend over. Sorry, just being a bit cynical."

They laughed and watched as a small diminutive sailor wrestled his overstuffed sleeping bag and a set of golf clubs up the brow. The site became more amusing, when the golf balls begin rolling out of an unzipped pocket of the oversize golf bag. Golf balls were bouncing all over the quarter deck. A couple managed to bounce over the side and into the Cooper River, while yet another, was bouncing its way merrily back down the brow towards the pier. For a few brief moments there was lighthearted pandemonium.

The quick action of the quarterdeck watch, and a few observers, brought things back under control once again. This was not accomplished though, until many comments had been voiced, especially about this being the future for all the remaining balls in the bag. The frustrated and embarrassed sailor gathered up the remaining balls, what was left of his composure, and continued on to his berthing area.

The time was now 0930 and the word was passed over the ships annunciation system, known as the '1-MC,' "All visitors are requested to leave the ship at this time; the ship will be getting underway in 30 min." The next word passed over the 1-MC was, "Now go to your stations all special sea and anchor details."

The tempo in activities increased, emotions ranged from dread, to pleasant anticipation. The time for deployment was at hand. Final preparations are now being made. Phone lines were disconnected; potable water that had been provided from the pier was now disconnected. From this moment on, the ships evaporator system would have to make all the freshwater that would be needed on board. The evaporator system takes in salt water from the sea, then converts it to fresh water. This is one of Robinson's jobs as the senior machinist mate on board, along with the air-conditioning-refrigeration and chilled water systems on board the ship.

Finally the brow was removed, and the last remaining link with the pier is now the doubled mooring lines. The last tugboat nudged alongside, and the crew affixed its working lines to the bits located on the ship's main deck, the word came down from the bridge. "Single up all lines!" This signaled the removal of the doublings of the mooring lines, leaving only one single line from each of the six stations holding the ship to the pier.

The next word severs all physical ties for the next nine months. "Take in all lines." As this was done the tugs begin to chop and turn the water. They periodically began tooting their horns and whistles, signaling their recognition of orders given by the harbor pilot now on the ships bridge. The pilot would remain on the bridge of the ship, and would be responsible for a safe transit down the channel, through the Charleston Harbor. The pilot is in control of the ship, until he departs the vessel at the end of the channel.

As the last line cleared, the Boatswain Mate blew the handheld whistle and passed the word "underway, shift colors." This whistle was more like a referee's whistle used in basketball games, not the regular boatswain pipe. The bo'sns pipe would be used from now on, prior to announcing, all words passed over the 1-MC. Many ships captains preferred using the pipe while underway. From now, until the ship returned in nine months, this would alert the crew to listen up, to the 1-MC.

*Shift Colors* announced the signal to strike the national ensign from the Flagstaff aft, and hoisted it on the gaff. The gaff is an extension from main mast. The gaff is where it would fly during all normal underway periods.

Sailors all manned the rails, up and down the sides of the ship on all topside decks. Some tearfully waving goodbye to family and friends on the pier as the ship slipped into the Cooper River channel and turned the bow seaward. The remaining family members and friends gathered at the end of the pier and waved goodbye to their loved ones as the ship moved slowly down the river. Almost everyone remained at the end of the pier; visually they became smaller and smaller as viewed by the sailors from the deck of the ship. Soon the pier is out of sight.

Unassisted by any tugboats, the USS Mount Mitchell had cast off all lines, and now moving seaward down the Cooper River on her own. As the ship turned towards the two steel bridges spanning the Cooper River connecting Charleston and Mount Pleasant, some sailors (old salts) began to look up at the mast, pointing at the bottom of the Grace Memorial Bridge. "It ain't go-nah clear," said some of the seasoned sailors, trying to put fear in the hearts of those (Boot Camp) or less experienced ones. "I think the tide is wrong," Commented another one of the old salts. A few of the boots scurried for cover. This spurred laughter from all those instigating the prank.

Observing the visual effect, while standing on the deck of a ship passing under the bridge, gives the illusion that the clearance is much less than what it really is. It does appear the mast will strike the bridges, when actually there is a good 25 feet of clearance, between the very tallest mast on the ship, and the bottom of the bridge.

This also offers a spectacular sight for those travelers crossing the bridges at this particular time.

The transit took the ship past Patriots Point Naval Museum, forts Moultrie and Sumter, but most interestingly to Phil and Gail, standing at the rail side-by-side, downtown Charleston, and the battery. Yes the battery, with its cannons, cannonballs, mortars, monuments, and history, but most of all recollection of that first passionate kiss.

Phil unconsciously placed his hand on Gail's and with a gentle squeeze, looked at her and smiled tenderly, "That place will always be special to me."

"You will always be special to me," she said.

The Mount Mitchell slipped quietly from Charleston Harbor; leaving behind priceless memories, of one special night, but still ahead, *The Mediterranean Cruise 1984.*

# CHAPTER 8

**SEVERAL DAYS HAD NOW** gone by, and the Mitchell's crew had settled into their daily routines that would become a way of life for the next nine months; at least routine while underway.

The ship's crew had not yet had the opportunity to visit a port and taste that first liberty overseas. After fourteen plus days at sea crossing the Atlantic in route to the Mediterranean; as a general rule, sailors tended to get a little rowdy in the first liberty port letting off steam.

This topic had become daily discussion in the Wardroom and Chiefs Mess. The general consensus of action, was to come down hard on anyone fouling up on the beach, thereby setting up an early standard of expectation of behavior while on liberty.

The CO had been making announcements on the 1- MC concerning expected behavior and making it clear just how he would respond to anyone who wished to go his/her own way.

The announcement of a terrorist bombing in Jerusalem on 2 April was also a major point of concern. Forty eight people had been injured in a shopping center bombing at the hands of terrorist. Most thought it was the Islamic Jihad.

Since the Mediterranean area had become more difficult in regards to terrorism, the U.S. Navy ships are required to enforce a buddy system for all sailors going to shore. This simply requires any sailor going on shore, must have at least one other person with them the entire time they are off the ship.

The requirement isn't a great problem for most of the crew, because the teaming up process had already begun during the transit. Although most of the matchups are, male with male, female with female, there were some who, by nature, chose the, male-female, relationship. Some folks just stick together in a group such as 4, 5, 6 or 10. After all, the thinking is that there is safety in numbers.

Not much is said about these arrangements, as long as the relationships did not interfere with work and there are no direct supervisor worker pairings.

Phil and Gail had chosen to be running mates. For them this seemed to be the, natural and ideal situation. Both of them are single and had no one waiting for them stateside.

Spain was just one day away and the crew begins looking forward to some time off. To get away just for a few hours, relaxing on the beach; yes, this will be great.

Some planned to visit the local saloon known as the Texas bar. Here a person is able to get, American-style food and plenty of cold American beer. The homemade Texas chili at the bar is known throughout the Navy as the best east of Amarillo.

Many of the younger sailors talk as if this is the only Texas bar in the Med (Mediterranean). However, the veterans know better. There are more Texas bars in the world, and especially in the Mediterranean, than there are camels in Arabia.

Phil and Gail also are looking forward to a little time to spend alone. The Atlantic transit had been long and tiring. They were both feeling the effects of the 16 hour days during underway periods.

Their work schedules had been such that they hadn't had much time to talk other than strictly business. The ship had been involved in three underway replenishments or "UNREPS," as they were known. During these unrep evolutions, Phil was on deck, and in the ship's magazines supervising and tracking the movement of ammunition. Gail on the other hand was busy keeping her part of the ammo working parties moving in a safe and efficient manner. She was a safety observer; this was considered a collateral duty, one added to her normal office duties. Collateral duties are assigned to almost everyone, and help make it possible for the ship to continue to operate safely. Keeping a ship the size of Mount Mitchell going is an all hands evolution, a team effort. There isn't much opportunity for Phil and Gail to discuss the problem of how to approach, and handle the situation of Allen and her stable of young women.

# CHAPTER 9

**THE SHIP IS IN** sight of land, now only about ten miles from The Straits of Gibraltar. Approaching closer with each turn of the screw; the crew begins feeling the large rolling ground swells forming beneath the ship's hull.

The surges and size of the swells are caused by the shallowing of the water; in other words, the bottom was getting closer to the surface.

A few supertankers are at anchorage, waiting for clearance to enter the Mediterranean.

The ship moved slowly through the straits, with Gibraltar on the port side (Europe) and Tangier (Africa) on the starboard side. Every ship sailing out the Mediterranean in history, passed through these straits; on their quest to discover the new world.

Many of the crewmembers stand topside to observe this moment. It will be nine months before they see this again.

The Mt Mitchell continues on toward Palma, and there their first port-of-call.

While the ship makes its approach to the anchorage in Palma Spain, the crew is busy making all preparations for entering port.

The ship was given final clearance to enter port just the night before. This was somewhat of a political game that the Spanish government was playing considering the initial clearance had been granted for the port visit several months before. Just another way of letting Uncle Sam know, just who was in charge in this area.

Most members of the ship's crew didn't know, or even care about the politics, or the policies involved in getting them in and out of the ports they were scheduled to visit. Most didn't follow the Mediterranean politics in general.

Phil watched the boatswain mates rig the accommodation ladder over the side, a process that will be repeated each time the ship anchors.

Chief Allen approached. "How's progress senior? Think we'll be able to get on the beach soon?"

He answered, "Yeah, looks as if these guys really know what they're doing."

Allen moved closer alongside him, and so close as to feel the heat radiating from his arm. She looked up at him and said, "My, you're warm, been here in the sun all day, or are you just naturally hot all the time?"

"I have my moments" Phil answered reassuringly.

"I guess you and Blondie will be going over tonight and soak up some of the local culture." She remarked, in a sort half question, have statement manner.

Phil looked at her for a moment, and then nodded with "Yeah, want to come long?"

This totally caught her off guard. She stood there for a few seconds dumbfounded before she could answer. "Well, I think threes a crowd, but I'll take a rain check if you don't mind." She noticed Gail approaching them and decided to excuse herself, "I'll talk to you later Senior, and plan on a night out on the town for the two of us." She walked away.

Gail came up and posted herself by Phil. "What was Madam X up to?" Gail asked.

Phil said coyly. "Oh not much, she was sorry she couldn't go with us tonight, something about three being a crowd."

Gail looked up at him with a chuckle in her voice, "You actually asked her to go out with us tonight?" Then the chuckle turned serious. "What would you have done if she would've said yes; and then?"

Phil looked into her sparkling eyes and said, "She would never say yes as long as you're around. She doesn't like to be overshadowed by personality and beauty such as yours. I also overheard her tell Chief Robinson she was going to get a hotel room for a couple of days. So you see I knew there were two reasons she would not go. Therefore I asked. I don't want anything, or anyone to come between us and a nice evening we have planned."

Gail smiled and patted Phil on the arm "Just mind that you don't go trying to get too brave and too smart. Madam X is weaving her web and I don't like the direction she's weaving it."

Phil laughed and reassured her he would watch his step. Gail had her sights on him and he didn't mind one bit. Phil had begun to fall in love with her from the moment they met, but he thought she would be out of reach for him. Things seem to be going well for the two of them at this point, but would it last. This was his greatest fear. After all, with the experiences of his first marriage, he intended to take things a bit slower.

# CHAPTER 10

**GAIL AND PHIL WERE** sitting at the table in the Chiefs mess planning their evening on the town when, in walked Allen and Robinson. Both Phil and Gail thought this to be a strange pairing. They knew of Robinson's expressed feelings about Allen.

Robinson poured a cup of coffee for himself and then one for Allen. She had already taken a seat. "Here you are Chief," He said, holding the cup of coffee out to Allen.

Gail turned to Phil, and in a rather sheepish manner said, "Looks as if you were outflanked by Robbie."

"No" Phil answered "I think what we have here is an attempt to get into the enemy's camp; infiltration at work in front of our eyes."

"We'll see," replied Gail "she's a slick operator." "I just hope Robbie is careful. Did he tell you about this before today?"

"Not a single word, but I think he wants to solo for a while. He knows more about her and her background probably than anyone else on board. He was in Washington DC, while she was in Moscow. If he can't get next to her, maybe he can ferret out some information about the overall organization, or whatever it is they're doing. That sure would make it easier to stop her before she gets into full swing." Phil was being optimistic and Gail knew this.

"I just hope she doesn't catch on to it. You know as well as I do, how much of a snake she is." Gail's contempt for Allen was obvious. She had never gone out of the way to hide her feelings. Phil tried to reassure her while at the same, time harboring concerns of his own.

Gail said to Phil "See you at dinner?"

He replied "Yeah wouldn't miss it for the world." They both departed to their respective bunk rooms and began to get ready for their first night in Palma.

Each of them was a little apprehensive about Robbie's going on the limb by himself, especially when such a move could jeopardize his career or much more.

# CHAPTER 11

**THE MOUNT MITCHELL WAS** swinging lazily on its anchor in Palma Harbor. The draft of the ship is too deep to allow it to go pier side anywhere in the port. The fact that she was an ammunition ship, made the port authorities want to keep her a little further out in the harbor as well.

The liberty sections were standing topside awaiting arrival of the water taxis. The ships boats provide some transportation back and forth for the crew, but as a token of goodwill, the ship also hired civilian water taxis. These taxis run from the dock of Palma every hour on the hour up until midnight. All hands are excited about their first liberty, and those who are not on duty, lined up and waited for the trip ashore.

Phil touched Gail's shoulder, "Our ride is here," as a boat pulled alongside. They made their way down the accommodation ladder and stepped into the water taxi as it rose and fell slightly with the comings and goings of the shallow waves. Taking their seats, then moving closer to one another allowed more room for others, and allowed them to make contact without undue attention. This trip into Palma, Mallorca was going to be great, or at least they thought at the time.

The water taxi reached the landing and everyone debarked. The two walked along the waterfront, enjoying the view of the city; laughing and enjoying the beauty that Palma offers as they mused about how nice it must be, to be able to afford one of the fine yachts that are moored there. Palma is a playground for many of the rich and famous from around the world. The harbor has many fishing vessels as well. Many of the residents of the island make, their living fishing the Mediterranean waters.

The couple stopped to gaze across the shimmering water; Phil laid his hand on Gails and said "This reminds me of the battery." Gail moved closer, remembering that special night they had shared. She looked up and smiled, her voice broke the silence as she reminded him, "We have many of our other shipmates out here tonight, so we had better move on, and find a restaurant before we end up in trouble."

He agreed, and they departed that particular spot, moving off in search of food. They walked along the narrow streets, and then a familiar voice sang out.

"Hey Senior, come on in and have a cold one with us." It was gunner Fitzpatrick.

Phil looked at Gail seemingly to ask if she would mind; but she responded before he could say anything, "Let's go and visit for a while." The two of them entered, cheers went up all around.

Gail shouted over the noise of the rowdy crowd, "My God Phil, it looks as if half the crew is here!" They made their way across the bar room floor, sliding in and out around tables and chairs, talking to the crew members as they made their way through the roomful of happy patrons. Finally making it to the bar, the owner Jimmy greeted them, "Welcome to the Texas bar, what will ya'll have?"

Phil glanced at Gail "Name your poison, it's on me." "Gin

and tonic will work." Phil looked at Jimmy and ordered, "Two gin and tonics mate." Jimmy gave the thumbs up and started mixing the drinks. Philip fell into Gail's soft, blue, intoxicating eyes and whispered, "I must warn you, gin turns me into a Casanova."

Gail raised her eyebrows and was about to comment when Jimmy returned with the drinks. "Drinks are on your shipmate over there." Jimmy pointed to the right in the direction of Fitzpatrick. They each picked up her glasses and raised them in his direction, a sort of long distance toast. Fitz responded with a salute, "Enjoy!" They sipped their drinks and smiled at each other.

Gail said "Here's to you, Casanova."

He grinned, "Here's to you my lady."

Fitzpatrick approached them, "Chief Robinson and Chief Allen dropped in about an hour ago."

Gail's smiled turned cold. "Where did they go?" She asked.

"They said something about going up on the hill where the restaurants and hotels are. They said they were going to get dinner and do some dancing. From the way Chief Robinson sounded, he was already on cloud nine. He was talking about doing the horizontal dancing. He was feeling pretty good." This was alarming to Phil.

He looked at Gail and posed the question, "What the hell is he doing?"

"I don't know, I really don't know, but I don't like it." They finished their drinks, bought two rounds for the guys, and made their way out and into the evening air.

"I hope Robbie knows what he's doing," Gail said, "That bitch will ruin everything for him, I thought he was married?"

"Separated, awaiting the divorce." Phil tried to reassure her, "I'm sure he'll watch his step. Just wish he would've filled us in on what he was doing, and what he was up to prior to taking any kind of action."

They walked up the street until the Hotel Valparaiso came into view. Traffic was clear and no pedestrian traffic around; partially hidden by a wall, they had a few seconds alone and they embraced. The kiss was long and passionate, but shortly it was interrupted by the sound of a bell, announcing the arrival of a young boy on his bicycle passing them. They recovered, readjusted themselves, and continued the walk.

"I need food," Phil whispered, "and maybe some dancing too."

Gail held tightly to his arm as they walked into the hotel lobby. They followed the managers direction to the restaurant area located on the first level. The maître d' greeted and seated them at a table overlooking the city, but with a limited view of the harbor.

"Look Phil," Gail said excitedly, "you can, just barely, see the ship from here."

The Mt Mitchell was sitting quietly in the harbor; all of the topside lights were now on and shining brightly. The lights glittered like sprinkles reflecting across the water. "She looks so peaceful from here." "My, gosh, all those lights are spectacular." Gail said.

"Yes they are, but not nearly as spectacular as the radiance in your face at the moment."

She turned to him and said "I guess I'm just a happy camper right now. Have another gin and tonic, Casanova?"

"You know Phil; you stir feelings in me that never existed before we met." His hand moved across the table and caressed hers. Her heart was racing, and her mind was filled with questions. She was about to speak when they were interrupted.

"May I take your order please?"

Suddenly they remembered where they were, and quickly adjusted their posture. "Yes, thank you. You speak perfect English." Phil said.

"I would hope so" said the waiter "I'm from Iowa, although I don't know about the perfect part. I work here at night; I attend the university during the day: exchange student."

Gail asked, "What do you recommend for two hungry world travelers? What's the chef specialty?"

The young waiter laughed lightly "What's his specialty? Fussing at the cooks and the other waiters; no, really he does great paella."

He smiled at the quizzical expression on their faces, and explained, "That is a combination of prawns, muscles, rice with saffron, he specializes in that, and I might add it comes on a rather romantic arrangement."

Phil answered quickly "American man, bring it on my friend, and don't tarry."

He looked towards Gail and she was smiling with approval.

The meal was fantastic, combined with the ambiance of the restaurant, all seemed so romantic.

As the two were finishing dinner, the waiter appeared with a bottle of white wine.

"Compliments of the chef; he appreciates seeing people in love, and enjoying his specialty." They looked in the direction of the kitchen; there stood the well-rounded Chef, smiling and nodding at them.

"What makes him think we are in love?" Gail asked.

"It's written all over both of your faces, even a blind person could tell."

They both raise their glasses that the waiter had now filled with the white wine, and toasted the chef. He smiled blew them a kiss, and returned to the kitchen.

They turned back to each other; Phil spoke "To you, my love." His eyes were deeply searching into Gail's dancing blue eyes'; she in turn, was searching his, as if trying to look into his inner most being and see his thoughts.

"Here's to love." She said the words almost without realizing her lips were moving. Something was stirring in her heart, something she had been dealing with, more and more whenever she was with him. The wine was now gone, and they joined a few other patrons on the dance floor. Dancing without talking gazing into each other's eyes, they were lost in the present. They knew they had fallen in love.

Time and events rushed by. As if transported by magic, they found themselves in a sixth floor room surrounded by Spanish paintings of bullfighters, and senoritas dancing and twirling. In the corner by the balcony doors, waited the king-size bed with large fluffy pillows.

They moved to the balcony, standing there they were wrapped in each other's arms, kissing passionately, and the feeling of excitement building wildly.

Gail pulled gently away and turned to go inside. Phil, standing alone, looked out over the harbor. With the now elevated view from the sixth floor, he could see the ships lights reflecting on water. Quivering on the water's surface, the reflections seemed to match frequency of his pounding heart. He wondered in his deepest thoughts, if this was supposed to be happening, were they ready emotionally.

Gail's soft voice calling to him broke into his thoughts: "Phil, I'm chilly come hold me."

He turned to see a shadow in the night. There in front of him stood the stunning sight that only his imagination had conjured up before. She was there, arms stretched out, nothing on but a gold chain around her neck. The chain he had given her just days before, while they were crossing the Atlantic.

His eyes beheld an entirely different view from the shapely uniformed person he had been accustomed to seeing. "Come in Phil" she whispered. As he moved to her, he could feel the throbbing emotion inside. They embraced, and she started to systematically undress him, until they were both standing completely nude. There in the subdued light of the room, he lowered her gently on the king sized bed, and placed gentle kisses on her body from head to toe. This he repeated over and over until she too was filled with emotion. His warm hands moved over her in the silence of the night. The light pressure of his touch caused her to respond.

"Slowly" she said "I want to savor this moment and remember it throughout eternity." By this time Phil had joined his body with hers, their lips were pressed together as if in a permanent bond.

Writhing, twisting, pushing, pulling and then the moment arrived. The great enormous outpouring of emotion, as they held each other so tightly, they continued to kiss holding onto each other, they drew out the entirety of the emotional moment. They lay there observing each other, kissing and embracing. Once again the passion grew. Phil had once again reached his full potential, and Gail was once again receiving him into her body. Heavy perspiration was now rolling off the two; the moisture was glinting and gleaming in the subdued light, as they were entangled the burning throes of their aggressive love making. They once again reached the pinnacle of emotional joy. Gail continued holding on to Phil as if their two bodies were one. Still the lips were pressing against one another. Phil opened his eyes, Gail looking at him; she seemed to be trying to read his soul in that moment. He whispered to her "I love you." "And I you" she said. While still clutching on to each other, they drifted off into a peaceful and blissful sleep.

## CHAPTER 12

**AS THE GENTLE MEDITERRANEAN** breeze moved across the hillside, the aroma of breakfasts wafted along with it, drifting gently into the bedroom. Gail had been awake for nearly an hour. She had taken her shower, and called room service for breakfast. Phil still asleep, remained completely motionless during the entire time. She stood in the balcony doorway, taking advantage of the warm breeze which aided in drying her golden hair, she watched him sleep. Moving towards the bed she spoke gently to him, "Good morning lover." His eyebrows twitched, but his eyelids remained closed, his nostrils flared, "What is that glorious aroma?"

"It's our breakfast being prepared, and momentarily to be delivered. I called room service." Gail answered, as she moved her index finger around Phil's lips encircling his nose.

"Not that smell," he retorted, "The smell, the aroma, of fresh flowers on the morning, and the tantalizing fragrance of romance, surely there are..." He stopped short of finishing his prose, opened his eyes, and looked directly into the lovely smiling face. "My word, the most beautiful morning flower I should ever hope to see."

She had moved gracefully to the bed where he was still lying half covered by the rumpled, wrinkled sheet. She caressed his head in her hands, moving closer their lips met in the brief but passionate kiss. She pulled back as there was a knock at the door.

"That will be breakfast my love," she said.

Phil answered with "Just as luck would have it."

Following breakfast, he showered and dressed for the day. They were prepared for a morning of fun and sightseeing around the city. "Let's take the stairs." Gail suggested. They descended the stairs, arm-in-arm, into the lobby. At the halfway point she noticed a great deal of commotion coming from the street in front of the hotel. There was a police van, the shore patrol, and an ambulance there.

They pushed their way through the crowd Gail's hand tightened around Phil's arm.

"Oh-my-God!" Phil whispered as the two stood there staring down at a familiar face.

The shore patrol officer stood beside them, "Whatever possessed him to do that?" He said.

"Do what?" Gail asked, as she began shaking in disbelief. The officer responded with, "Get so wasted, that he thought he could walk the railing; seven damn stories. Can you believe this crap? I better get started; this one is going to be a mother." Realizing what he had said the Shore Patrol Officer modified his statement by saying "You know we've got to get to the bottom of this because we owe it to this guy to find out what went wrong here."

Still horrified, they turned away from the crumpled corps of Chief Robinson that now lay motionless. Tears welling up in both of them, anger more in Phil than anything.

The two were now experiencing an emotion quite different from the one they had felt earlier. "It was that damn bitch Allen; I know she had something to do with this!" Gail had tried to hold back her anger, but the strain was overpowering her sensibilities. "The bitch will pay for this; the bitch will pay for this, I know she's behind this." By now a steady stream of tears and sobbing, made coherent words impossible, her breathing was increasingly difficult. They stood there looking around the scene, silently searching. The knowledge they had of the situation was enough at that time, they thought, to put a stop to Pat Allen once and for all; but, would that be the case?

# CHAPTER 13

**GAIL REGAINED HER COMPOSURE.** She began to ask questions from anyone she thought may have witnessed the tragedy. Phil was busy gathering any information from the officials on the scene. He noticed the unusual blood pattern around Robinsons head, and was pointing this out to the person whom seemed to be in charge.

At that moment a voice from behind him interrupted, "Have much experience investigating crime scenes?"

Phil turned to see a man in a blue Polo shirt with the letters N.I.S. embroidered on the left breast. "Crime scene?" Phil asked.

"Yes" answered the agent, "I have declared this a crime scene and I'll have to ask, what interest you have in the Vic?"

"I am Senior Chief Mattingly, and Chief Robinson, your, 'Vic' is, was, my shipmate and friend. We are from the Mt Mitchell, the ship at anchorage in the harbor."

"So you and the young lady are together?" asked the agent, pointing his notepad in Gail's direction.

Phil glanced toward her, "Yes, we came upon the scene at the same time." The agent extended his hand to Phil.

"Sorry about your friend, I'm Agent James Love, Naval

Investigative Service. I have spoken to Chief Cornell already; she is quite upset as well. She thinks there may be a connection between this and another situation onboard. Can you enlighten me on this?"

Phil's brow wrinkled as he carefully formulated his answer, "The last time we saw Chief Robinson alive, he was preparing to leave the ship with Personnel Chief, Pat Allen. That is about all the concrete knowledge I have."

"I see," agent Love said. "Well the blood pattern you noticed as being unusual was caused by a gunshot to the head; know anything about that?"

"My God no!" answered Phil. "Who the hell would kill him? He's just a career sailor." Agent Love studied Mattingly for a few seconds. "Here is my card Senior, I am out of Rhoda, just happened to be here on an unrelated case, so I caught this one. If you can think of anything else I should know about, please contact me. I'll be here for the next couple of weeks before I have to head back to Rhoda. I will visit with your CO later today."

"You can count on us." Phil said.

Gail joined the two and asked, "Any signs of Allen?"

"Apparently Robinson was the only one in the room from where he fell." Agent Love informed them, "No signs of anyone else being in there with him. Please, if there is anything else you know that could help in this case, I need to know."

"We will definitely be in touch with you Agent Love," Gail said.

# CHAPTER 14

**GAIL AND PHIL DECIDED** to return to the ship to find out if anyone had knowledge or knew of any reason for Robinson's senseless murder. They especially, wanted to speak with the Captain; and to find out if Allen could have had a hand in the killing of their friend.

Arriving back onboard, they were staggered, by the sight that greeted them. There on the quarterdeck, stood Chief Allen, dressed in khaki uniform and seemingly waiting for them.

Allen greeted them, "Glad to see you two back safe, we were about to send someone to find you, but the *beach guard* radioed you were in the water taxi, on your way back."

"What the hell do you know Allen?" asked Gail, in a gruff but subdued voice. She was in Allen's face, only about one inch from her nose. Phil took her arm and said, "Not here, save it for the mess, there you can kick her ass if you want, but not here in the open."

Allen, in more of a quiet and submissive tone responded. "Do not say another word, follow me."

Phil questioned, "Follow you where?"

"The Captain's cabin." Allen headed off in that direction, followed by two bewildered and frustrated individuals.

Arriving at the cabin door, Allen turned, looked at the two of them, but didn't say a word. She turned and knocked twice and listened, "Enter!" was the response from inside. Allen opened the cabin door; the Captain greeted them.

"Please come in, have a seat, we have some information to process." Gail was, still fired-up and about to stare a hole through Allen. Commander Worrell, noticing the tension, started by saying, "First of all let me introduce the two of you, to FBI Agent Samantha Langston." The two looked at the Captain in disbelief, then slowly and simultaneously rotated their heads and eyes toward the person they had thought to be Chief Allen.

"I am terribly sorry for having to keep you two in the dark, but this was the plan from the bureau prior to me taking this assignment. I am heartbroken about Chief Robinson. Nothing like this was supposed to happen, I brought him back to the ship last night, he was feeling the effects of wine, and a few mixed drinks. He was trying to get me to stay overnight with him in a room he had rented earlier. I know this is the kind of behavior everyone would expect of Allen, but not me, the FBI Agent. I guess you might say the cover was working the way it was supposed to; or maybe too well. I thought he had gone to bed, so I turned in for the night. From what I learned this morning, he later gathered up a change of clothes, and went back ashore with a group of people. I figure he just blended in with them. The next thing that we know the *beach guard*, is informing us about the situation at the hotel."

Phil asked "Just what is your assignment here anyway?" Gail was still trying to get a grip on the overall situation.

"Where do the female sailors, supposedly working for you fit in?" asked Gail.

"They are all plants, sent here to help make the story more believable. Most are field agents in training, under my direction."

"That explains why no one could pin anything on you, because nothing ever happened." Gail said.

"Precisely, said Langston, "give the appearance of impropriety, and let the people's imagination run with it. Each complaint that did get filed was noted, stamped, and tucked away in a case folder at the bureau."

"As for your question Phil, the simple answer is *sarin gas*."

"Sarin Gas!" Phil repeated in shock.

"Yes, a shipment of five projectiles loaded with the toxic gas, scheduled for destruction, was hi-jacked six months ago in Belgrade. The terrorist plan is to transfer the gas back to the U.S. onboard a navy ship. Once offloaded, and while in transit to the final destination, the terrorist plan to re-hi-jack the finished product. Then they would distribute the gas among their sleeper cells around the country. Following all that, it would be used for a coordinated attack on highly populated areas, such as sporting events, subways, air terminals and congress."

Phil asked, "Just how do they plan on getting it onboard a ship, especially a navy ship?"

"Simple but intricate," Langston explained. "Retrograde ammo going back to Yorktown, Virginia. Gun ammo as you know is routinely returned to the US for reworking. The CIA has informed us that, the projectiles that had contained the gas were found in a ditch; by a farmer. The ditch was beside the field he was plowing. The location is just outside Bosnia. The projectiles had been emptied of their contents. The gas is sealed in glass vials designed to break open when the projectile detonates. Coincidently a small batch of 5" propelling charges turned up missing from inventory at the NATO site in Madeira, Portugal, a small island offshore from the Straits of Gibraltar. Twelve charges in total were reported as unaccounted for."

Gail commenced a summation of events, "Yes, I see what they

plan on doing," as she turned toward Phil to explain, "They dump out enough powder to create a space in the powder canister, large enough for the vials to fit in. Then they probably wrap the canisters in some sort of cushioning foam, and backfill the container with a portion of the powder that was just emptied out, then reinstall the nose plug, piece-thingy, and put it back in the shipping case."

Phil said "I was with you up to the *thingy* part, that piece is called the mouth plug and they are tough to remove and replace without doing serious damage to them."

The Captain spoke up, "I think these people, whoever they are, are clever enough to figure that part out."

"Where do they plan to assemble all of this? And how do they plan to get the ammo back into the system?" asked Phil.

Langston spoke up, "Word from the CIA is; it's done already. They are trying to put the links together now to trace it. The bad guys have sympathizers working within the system. By the way Phil, the ship that the terrorist are planning to use is, Mt Mitchell."

"Well, all we have to do is reject any shipments of that ammo, surly we can't have that much going back." Phil suggested.

The Captain explained "We have 500 rounds from Naples, and 400 from Ashdod."

Langston continued, "We are going ahead with all on loads. As of this morning, we think the terrorist believe their plan is undetected. The shipment will go back with us, and be unloaded in Charleston as if all is normal. There it will be prepped for shipment by rail to Yorktown. Somewhere between Charleston and Yorktown, we believe an ambush will occur; we will be ready for them."

"Where does the killing of an innocent man come into play?" asked the Captain.

"At the moment Captain, that part has me baffled, unless

somewhere, there is a leak. Another reason I'm here is; we think the terrorist have a contact onboard."

"Agent Langston" Phil asked "where do we go from here?"

"I would suggest that you two continue on with your activities ashore. I have to get with my backup people on the ship. Keep your eyes and ears open, and at least now, you can concentrate on someone, other than me."

"Captain," what about Robinson's body?" Phil asked.

"His remains will go to Rota, and will be prepped for return stateside. The XO (Executive Officer) will put together a memorial service for him; it will be between here and Naples. For the love of God shipmates, watch your six!" Worrell looked at each of them and said "Unless you have something else, that's all I have for now, keep me informed," With that, the three of them departed the cabin.

Gail turned to agent Langston, "How about a cup of coffee?"

Samantha gave her a wink and said, "Stuff it, Blondie."

They all knew that appearances from before would have to be maintained. Somehow they trusted that there would be less actual tension. Now they could concentrate on the task at hand; while maintaining the façade of antagonism.

# CHAPTER 15

**THE TWO WENT BACK** to the mess to freshen up, and pack some clean clothes. The plan was to go back to the hotel room, and use it as a base of operation for the next few days. The Captain had removed them from any duties onboard for the remainder of the port visit.

Phil and Gail both knew that once back in the room they would be remembering the passion from the night before; because it still stirred within both of them. But they each knew a repeat of the night before would have to wait. As for the weekend ahead of them, they planned on using the time to look for clues surrounding the death of their friend Robinson.

The water taxi reached the dock, Phil noticed NIS Agent Love standing under a makeshift shed. As they stepped off of the boat onto the dock, Love met them.

"Had a hunch you'd be back, got a message from the CO. He indicated to me that you two might come looking for clues. He wanted me to look after you, and keep you out of trouble. Have any idea what trouble he may be talking about?"

"I think the Captain is referring to our dogged and determined attitudes; when we dive, we dive deeply." Phil stated.

Agent Love chuckled, "Matter of fact that is just what he did say. This is deeper than just a random killing. You both probably put that together after your conversation with Langston and the CO."

"You know about her?" Gail asked.

"I was *read in* after the murder, I understand now what you were referring to when you said there was a *situation onboard the ship*. I often get sent out without all the information pertaining to a case. The Mediterranean is crawling with spies, and one slip of the tongue, well…, could be your last. Let me take you to the hotel, we can look at the room together. I found something that might interest you. Senior, you said you have some experience in investigations."

"Yes," Phil said hesitantly "I spent some time with *the company*."

"Ah-yes, the agency." Love retorted in a half smarmy manner.

Gail's focus locked on him. "THE CIA? You worked for the CIA?"

"Keep it low," warned Love. "Ears all around, remember."

"Yes, I did do some investigations, small but meaningful."

"You never once mentioned this to me." Gail said heatedly.

Love cut in, "I think there is a certain Senior Chief in hot water!"

Phil transferred his stare over to Love. "What do you mean by that?"

"Face it Senior, it's all over both of your faces, I'll leave it there." He chuckled again and tuned away and headed up the steps, made of concrete and sea shells, to the car. "Come on you two, there is a crime scene that needs investigating."

# CHAPTER 16

**AGENT SAMANTHA LANGFORD WAS** preparing to go ashore. She was adapting Robbie's modus-operandi, to her own usage. She joined in with a group of excited sight-seers leaving together. This satisfied the *buddy system rule*.

The water taxi reached the dock, as the passengers debarked; she slipped away unnoticed. Sam headed for the Valparaiso.

Now standing outside the hotel, Samantha observed the balcony where Robbie had fallen, or had been thrown from, and the spot where his body came to rest. As she looked up she spotted Phil and Agent Love standing on the balcony. She signaled to Phil, he motioned for her to come up.

Love noticed her. "Is that Agent Langston?"

Phil smiled "The one and the same."

"Wow, she is a looker."

"She is single for all we know," Gail said. "But you know there has been a lot of deception around here lately."

"Phil rolled his eyes, "Look, I just didn't think it was important. It was a long time ago." "Didn't you think it was important enough to share with me?" Gail asked?

Sam walked into the room. "Sounds like you're in the dog house Senior. Can't be me this time."

"Well actually it is," said Love, as he extended his hand to her. "Agent James Love, NIS Rota."

"Agent Samantha Langston, FBI, please, call me Sam."

"It appears that I'm the only one here without a three letter designation, other than, USN." Gail smirked.

Sam, being quick of mind, looked at Phil "That explains the missing pages from your record, which agency?"

He answered, "CIA."

"Cool." said Sam. "Phil, some advice for you; if you are going to be in a serious relationship, you've got to be honest with your partner."

"Thank you!" Gail said, "We girls have to stick together."

"I never thought I'd see this day," Phil quipped.

The conversation turned back to evidence hunting, starting with a shell casing Love had found.

"This is what I wanted to show you guys." He held out a spent brass casing. "This was fired from a Parabellum. It has a unique taper to the brass, fired from a WWI era German Luger." It is a 7.65mm, 30cal bullet. Quite a few of them still around but…, this gun has been used before."

Sam asked, "What do you mean used before?"

"The hijacked projectiles, remember them? One of the Bosnian guards was shot with this type of round. We think the Jihad terrorist that did the hijacking, is the same shooter that killed Robinson."

"Where did you find the casing?" Sam inquired.

Love walked to the balcony, "See that flower pot directly under the balcony next door? It was in there. The lack of gunshot residue on the victim indicates the shot came from further than six feet. And the bullet that came from his head was a 7.65."

"I thought the Parabellum was a 9mm." Phil stated.

"That's true; it was made on the same frame style, but two different calibers. The 7.65 version is most likely one that is called the *Artillery*, longer barrel and a removable shoulder stock."

"Why would someone use a collector's piece for this?" asked Phil.

Love answered. "It's probably a stolen piece from some collector; or someone who served in WWII, hard to tell. These guns were used up to 1939 and after, when the Walther P38 was adapted for use in the German military. It's also easy to adapt a silencer onto them."

Sam stated. "Our terrorists are here, and if they have seen any of us, we are all targets." Everyone nodded their heads in agreement.

"We have a room here in the hotel," admitted Gail. "You're both welcome to come over and have some dinner and a drink. It's on the other side of the hotel overlooking the waterfront seventh floor. We can use it to operate from for the remainder of the port visit. I need to sort through everything that has happened in the last couple of days, it has been a long day for me I'll admit."

"Why don't you two go on and get some rest, maybe I can convince agent Langston into allowing me to treat her to dinner here in the restaurant. We can regroup tomorrow morning in the restaurant for breakfast"

Phil said, "That sounds like a plan; it has been a long day."

Sam said quickly "Shall we meet around 7 for breakfast?"

Gail answered, "Good idea, that's the plan." Each agreed, setting the wheels in motion for the next day.

Philip and Gail returned to their room, where they had room service bring dinner to them. After the meal, they lay across the king size bed next to each other. The events of the day had taken its toll on the two of them. While the cool Mediterranean air played across them; they held each other tightly and drifted into sleep.

## CHAPTER 17

**THE QUARTET OF INVESTIGATORS** met as scheduled for breakfast. Good mornings, and how did you sleep were the first questions of the day. Then Gail broke the ice.

"Did you two enjoy your evening?"

Samantha answered, "We did. It started with a wonderful dinner with a bottle of white wine provided by the chef, and then we took our turn on the dance floor, followed by a brief stroll around the hotel grounds."

James interjected "We turned in to our own rooms after that. We were well-fed and exhausted."

Phil asked, "Did the chef give a reason for the wine?"

Sam answered, "Something about, amore (ah-`more-re), I think is what he said. We didn't question his generosity, we simply enjoyed the wine."

With a broad smile on her face, Gail reached her hand across the table to Phil, "Does that sound familiar or what?"

Love and Langston looked at them with quizzical expressions on their faces.

"I'll explain later," Gail said to Sam, it's all good." "Did he say anything about the look on you faces?"

Sam answered, "Yes, as a matter of fact he did. We just brushed it off as maybe he had had some of his wine as well."

"We did?" James questioned.

The waitress approached with breakfast for four. "Just in time "Gail retorted, as she watched Sam moving nervously in her chair. The four enjoyed breakfast in relative quietness, although Phil and Gail kept looking at each other throughout breakfast, with sheepish grins on their faces.

The conversation turned back to the case.

"Was your waiter an American exchange student?" asked Phil.

"He was, said he was from Iowa, and there was a trainee with him" James answered, "a Middle Eastern man."

"I think we need to talk to the two of them" Phil stated. "One of them may have noticed something out of the ordinary. He is in class this morning so we will have to catch him when he comes in tonight."

Agent Love suggested they split up to lessen the probability of them being compromised, and just play tourist until about 1600 (4pm). "We'll meet back here, in the restaurant."

They broke into their two pairings, and headed out until time to interview the waiter.

---

Meeting back at the hotel restaurant, there was no sign of the waiter or the trainee. James went in search of the manager for information. He wanted to check the schedule and possible whereabouts of the trainee. He was met with shrugged shoulders, and bewilderment from management. They had no clue as to where either one of their employees were; but only that they were supposed to be at work.

Returning to the group, agent Love filled them in on the situation.

"No one seems to know where either the waiter or the trainee is at the moment, only that they are both supposed to be here. I did get the waiters name and address though. He lives just a few blocks from here on Carrer Porto. We can at least go there and maybe talk to him. His name is Quinton Parker. Here, I wrote the info down for you two, in case we get separated out of necessity; still a lot of your shipmates out here. Let's go."

While walking to the waiter's residence, Gail moved alongside Sam. "Back at the restaurant this morning, to let you know, the same thing happened to Phil and me our first night here."

Sam looked at her, "You mean…,"

"Yup, white wine, the look on our faces, people in love, everything. I think the chef may have noticed something between the two of you."

"That's ridiculous; there is nothing between Jim and me."

"Jim?" Gail responded. "How was the walk last night?"

"We had a pleasant stroll, and then he walked me back to my room."

"Did you kiss him goodnight?"

"Well yes, but just a light polite, thank you for a good evening kiss."

"Your heart beat increased didn't it? And a warming flush came over you?"

"What are you trying to say?" Sam asked. "That I'm falling for him, I haven't known him that long."

"Well, he is handsome, great body, seems to be a really good guy, and in your line of work, just saying. The subconscious knows before the conscience is aware."

"Your hormones are going to your head," Said Sam.

"Give it time Sam, give it time." Unbeknownst to them, a

similar conversation was occurring between James and Phil about 10 feet ahead.

They arrived at the address the hotel manager had given them. James knocked on the door. "Quinton Parker, NIS agent Love, we have some questions for you." There was no response. Again he knocked. "Quinton Parker, answer the door please.

Sam was looking through the wooden privacy fence. "The side door is open. Help me over." Phil gave her a boost over the wooden fence. She drew the small Walther PPK .380 she carried with her everywhere, and prepared to enter the side door. Less than ten seconds passed, she opened the door. "We're too late, he's dead."

"Dead!" Gail exclaimed, "What the hell is going on here?"

Agent Love eased into the two room apartment. He bent over as closely to the body as he dared, trying not to contaminate the crime scene; he wanted to examine it visually. "Assonated; appears to be a 30 caliber hole in his head, same as Robinson."

"The waiter in training, he may be our killer." Sam said.

"I think you are right on track Sam," Said Love. "We've got to call and notify the authorities, but we do not want to be here when they show up. Let them process the scene, we cannot get involved at this stage. We can't give up any info we have either." Love looked around at the other three and continued. "We will help where we can, for Quinton's sake, but to jeopardize our case would be folly."

The street was quiet, no foot or motorized traffic to be seen. Generally all family activities were conducted in the rear of the residences, the front facing the street simply for ingress and exit. Slowly they exited, careful not to leave a trace of their presence. Agent Love, fluent in Spanish, ducked into a phone booth to report the crime. They returned to the hotel.

"Jim, that picture you took last night of Quinton, the one you took with your Polaroid, do you still have it?"

"Yes, it's in my briefcase, why?"

"I believe the trainee could have been in the back ground."

Jim dug through his case. "Here they are."

"They?" Sam questioned. She started looking through the four pictures, three of which had her image in them. She glanced up at him, "Really?" She said.

"You make a good subject, I had to."

Sam looked over to Gail whom was smiling confidently. Sam displayed a faint smile and continued searching the pictures. "Here, that's him, over my right shoulder. We can put this on the wire to headquarters, and with any luck we will have a name, and profile within a day. I'll see if I can fax this from the hotel office. I believe this place is high end enough to have that service." She was off like a streak to fax the picture to FBI headquarters.

"Gail leaned in toward Love, "I think she likes you."

Love blushed, "Samantha is quite a woman."

"Well, you are a good guy too, and you deserve a good woman."

*Phil was about to bust-a-gut.* "James, just a few days ago she was ready to strangle Sam." "That's when I thought she was Chief Allen, not FBI Agent Langston. Anyway, think about it."

"I have." Love stated.

A few minutes later Sam came back through the door. "Success," She sighed "the numbers HQ gave me worked. My boss will pass the picture to the CIA. Jim I asked them to forward it to your office in Rota."

"Thanks, that was thoughtful."

She smiled, "Got to look out for each other here you know."

Phil asked, "Do you think Quinton was killed because he could identify our assassin?"

Sam spoke. "I believe the killer, may have thought so; this demonstrates how dangerous this guy is, and his willingness to kill anyone he believes can compromise his mission, whatever that is."

James said, "This guy was watching you a bit too much last

night Sam. I thought it was because he thought you were pretty or something but now I wonder...,"

"Pretty or something?" Gail said. "She's beautiful!"

"I meant nothing by that, she is beautiful," said Love.

Gail continued "That would be the real reason for the pictures, right?"

Sam looked at Phil "Ever felt like the third rail senior?" Phil chuckled.

James said. "Yes." Everyone froze in place and focused on him. "The answer to your question Gail; yes that is why I took the pictures, Samantha is beautiful." Silence was now the *white elephant* in the room for the next few moments.

Gail said to Phil, "I think we need dinner, don't you?" Gail tugged his arm "come on, I'm famished." Practically dragging him out of the room, she didn't slow down or look back. "Lock up if you two decide to join us for dinner." The door closed behind them.

"Wow, your attitude toward Allen sure has changed," Phil said.

"Philip, keep up, take notes or something; her name is Langston."

# CHAPTER 18

**AT BREAKFAST THE FOLLOWING** morning, Sam was sitting alone with her morning coffee. Gail came in. She began looking around as if in search of a missing piece to a puzzle. "Where's your fellow crime fighter?"

Sam looked up at her without Phil, "I could ask the same question."

"Yes, suppose so. How did the evening work out for you two? I know when Phil and I came back from dinner, you both were gone."

Sam smiled, "We walked down the hill to a small sidewalk restaurant, sat and had a quiet meal."

"And…?" Gail questioned.

"We came back to the hotel; and he escorted me back to my room.

That's it. Another simple *thank you for a nice dinner kiss*?"

"Yes, well maybe more than a nice dinner-kiss."

"Progress, we're making progress," said Gail. "By the way, where is Jim?"

"He's checking messages at the Consultant and going to Police HQ; snooping around trying to find out what he can about

Quinton's murder. The locals are unaware of his fluency in Spanish; he wants to keep it that way."

"Good idea; that could be helpful if the locals feel like they can talk freely around him. How about your sidekick? Did you devour him? You seemed to be famished last night."

"Just wanted to get out of your way, and no but I could, he's a great guy, and yes I am madly in love with him."

Sam touched her hand lightly, "I know sweetie, FBI you know. Jim and I had a conversation about the pictures, he asked if he could continue to see me after all of this is over."

"You said yes, didn't you?"

"Sort of; I guess."

"What do you mean by *Sort of*?"

"I told him I would be disappointed if he didn't."

Gail jumped up excitedly. She was giving Sam a big hug when Phil joined them.

His first words were, "It just keeps getting better and better."

Gail said in her loving voice, "Hush, sit down and eat your breakfast, we ordered for everyone."

A few short moments later James Love came in. He was proudly sporting a large manila envelope tucked tightly under his left arm.

"Good morning all. First breakfast, and then off to the OP Center. Our eyes only, good stuff in here." Jim tapped the envelope with his right index finger.

"Any hints for us?" asked Sam.

"Results from your photo; I went to the US Consulate; they have a direct line to Rota, and a secure line for faxing documents. Let's eat, I'm hungry."

"How can you be hungry at a time like this?" asked Sam.

"Easy, the walk over to the consulate, and don't forget the police station. All that walking so early in the morning can do that to a person."

Phil and Gail turned toward Sam, she responded, "Let him enjoy his moment, he's earned it." She then turned to Love. "Don't eat too slowly or I'll shoot you." Jim smiled then began his breakfast.

# CHAPTER 19

**ONCE THE QUARTET OF** investigators were back in the *op center* (Phil and Gail's room) Agent Love opened the envelope. He dropped a copy of the picture Sam had sent, and one the Bureau returned identifying their suspect.

"May I present to you, the trainee waiter, Mohamed Masawi; a member of the Islamic Jihad. They're known to be a Shia Islamist militia group headquartered in Beirut. Also they are responsible for the kidnapping of the CIA Station Chief, March 16 of this year; also responsible for the US Embassy bombing in Beirut 18 April last year, and the Marine barracks in Beirut October last year. There are more, but you get the idea of whom we are dealing with. This guy is our shooter; he is no one to toy with obviously. Question for you Sam, when you and Chief Robinson were out together the other night, did you notice anyone following you?"

"Not really; but there were many people prowling the streets that night, why do you ask?"

Love continued, "Last night after you returned to your room, I did some snooping around the bar and restaurant. Seems when Robbie came back the night before he was killed, he was bragging about being close to a big discovery on the ship. He gained the attention of our trainee waiter. I'm thinking he was killed because Masawi believed Robinson was referring to the transfer of the siren gas."

"My God," said Sam. "You mean he was murdered because of my cover?"

"I am afraid so Sam, but you are not to blame," said James.

Samantha dropped her head, "This has gotten out of hand, and I've got to do something about this, but what?"

Phil reassured her, "This is no one's fault but the bad guys Sam."

"But I do feel partially responsible for Robbie's death; you know allowing him to return to the beach." Sam said solemnly.

"I believe that is on Robbie," said Gail. "You can't blame yourself for what a grown person decides to take on for himself; there was nothing else you could have done."

Agent Love spoke up, "May I suggest we not split up any more, I think Masawi is following the ship around the Med. He is keeping a personal eye on the situation and he may be watching all of us along with every move we make. You guys have one more day in Palma, and then off to Naples. I'm having my room changed to the vacant one beside you Sam; I don't want to take any chances with this guy."

"I can handle myself," Sam protested.

"I know you can," stated James; "it's my safety I'm worried about." With that they all got a modicum of relief from the tension that was building.

"I have a great idea," James suggested. "Let's all jump in my rental car and drive over to the eastern side of Mallorca, town called Capdepera. Great Little café there named, Café Lorient great seafood and wonderful wine, you guys up for it?"

"Thanks for trying to cheer me up Jim; I'm not sure it'll help." Sam said sadly.

"Well one thing for sure agent Langston," Gail insisted, "it sure as hell won't improve by sitting around here moping. Look we've all lost a friend, and sooner or later we have to move on and do our jobs. Tomorrow is a new day, but right now I think Robbie would approve if we do this tonight in his memory. We will get the bad guys for him, and for us."

Sam shook her head in quiet agreement. "Where will you be while we are in Naples Jim?" Sam asked.

"I have your complete schedule and a case to solve. I'm not about to let you get all of the credit for solving this case by yourself. I will meet you in Naples."

Gail looked at Phil and winked. As they walked toward Jim's rental car, Samantha had taken hold of his hand. The foursome left for Capdepera, on the eastern shore of Mallorca. Upon their return they would be preparing for the ship's transit to Naples, and the memorial service for Robinson.

# CHAPTER 20

**THE AFTERNOON OF APRIL** 17th, the Mt Mitchell weighed anchor, and set a course a rendezvous point with other U.S. fleet units. The next twelve days they would be engaged in coordinated exercises with these fleet units deployed for this cycle. Most of the exercises were conducted for training purposes. Many events had taken place while in Palma, Spain, although they were there only a short period.

As promised, a memorial service for Machinist Mate Chief Richard Robinson was observed. The service was held on Sunday the twenty second of April 1984. The ships CH-46 helicopters were flown during the ceremony, and at the conclusion, a fly-by was performed with one of the Ch-46's peeling off, flying out about three miles and gaining altitude before returning to join the other. This was to represent the *"Missing Man"* tradition.

Following the memorial service, the Captain requested the three onboard newly formed inspectors join him in his at sea cabin.

Agent Langston proceeded to lead the group following behind the Captain. The Captain entered holding the door open for the entourage to enter.

"This is something I never want to have to do again," stated the

Captain. "It's always tough when you lose a member of your crew, but to lose one in this situation, is intolerable. Aside from the three agents you have under you agent Langston, is there anyone else that may want to strike out on their own trying to solve this fictitious situation we have created onboard?"

"No Captain." Sam answered quickly.

"No one else as far as we know sir." said Phil speaking for Gail as well.

"Good, let's keep it that way. This morning I received an eyes only message from CENTCOM (Central Command) that Special Forces had captured alive a member of the hi-jacking crew. His people believe he was killed in a raid near Beirut and unaware he was alive and being interrogated by U.S. agents. The CIA managed to extract some usable information from him that pertains particularly to us. The containers carrying the sarin gas are marked with a specific dent struck by a punch and the locking wire will be slightly different. How different can they be Senior Chief?"

Mattingly thought for a moment, "The only thing I can think of, off the cuff, is the stamp on the lead seal, type of wire, or direction of the twist on the wire."

"What do you mean by twist?" asked the CO.

Phil continued, "When the shipping containers leave the factory, the safety wire keeping the lid in place and making it tamper resistant, is twisted with a wire twist tool. The tool winds the wire in a counterclockwise direction then the lead seal placed over that and then stamped with an ordnance stamp. Generally speaking when that wire is twisted by hand, it is done clockwise twisting motion, just human nature. I've seen hundreds of them, and ninety five percent done by hand, are clockwise. One other thing Captain, the weight may be different. The entire shipping case and propelling charge together weigh 43.5lbs. The actual amount of powder is 21lbs. If we weigh them, there may be a difference; even a slight amount would be enough to set it aside. The factory quality control is extremely tight."

The Captain looked around at all of them and said, "We are taking on 500 charges this week in Naples. Will we have time to train some of the handling crew what to look for?"

"Yes we do Captain," Phil said. "We will start as soon as we leave here; I have a crew in mind."

"Great," said the CO. "Try to keep a tight lid on this, I don't want any word of what we are looking for to get out. The message also stated that all the ammo in question is on this Naples load. The Israelis were too tough for these guys to penetrate. "One other thing; watch out for one another in Naples. I don't want any more memorials."

"Yes Sir Captain." They each repeated; and with that, they all departed the quarters.

Gail asked, "Why don't we destroy the vials when we find them?"

"The purpose of all of this is to get to the root of the organization and take it out. We will find the gas, but as far as the Jihadist knows, they are pulling one over on us." Sam continued, "What we hope to gain is knowledge of the inner workings of the Islamic Jihad, also the locations of the sleeper cells in the U.S. So you see, this thing goes much deeper, and is more intricate, than just our small part of it. That is why we must not fail in our portion of the entire operation."

"When will the team come aboard to open these things and make them safe?" asked Gail. Phil spoke up, "The team is already here."

Gail looked at him with a wrinkled brow. "Where are they?"

"Phil, you really need to work on your communication skills." Sam said.

"You are looking at the team. I was with EOD (Explosives

Ordnance Disposal), Seal Team One in Vietnam. I used to disarm bombs and munitions for a living. That is the reason the captain requested my assignment directly from the Bureau of Personnel through the Pentagon. "I had a reputation for being the best."

"Had?" said Gail, "What do you mean by that?"

"Nothing really, I just haven't done it in a while. Just like riding a bicycle though, one never forgets."

"Only when you fall off a bicycle, you don't die!" stressed Gail. "Phil, I made my mind up a while back, I'm going where you go, and this sarin gas situation is not getting in my way. So start training, there is a lot I need to know."

Sam spoke, "I don't think arguing with her is going to help Phil, looks like you may have one on the line that you can't shake off."

Phil, while smiling, looked at Sam and said, "I don't believe I'd ever try."

"I had better get back to being Pat Allen before we get caught being nice to each other." "See you later," said Gail.

"Stuff it Blondie." Sam said as she smiled and walked away. Phil chuckled while shaking his head.

# CHAPTER 21

**18-APRIL-1984, THE SHIP IS** underway for Naples, Italy. Ahead, the on-load of the suspicious ammunition, and determining whether or not it had been tampered with. The next ten days would be spent at sea conducting scheduled operations and training. Periods between port visits were always used to keep the ship and crew in top operational readiness. This time however, Phil was busy training two of his best people to assist in finding the powder cases containing the sarin gas vials.

They were familiarizing themselves with all the various markings that were standard, to better able themselves with anything out of the ordinary, when it occurs. A special set of scales were set up for weighing each pallet of charges for when they arrive on board. One topside magazine was cleared of its contents and prepared for use in the staging of the suspect charges.

All of this would be accomplished as the shipment arrived aboard. The operation would be out of the sight of all crew members, except those involved in the ammo detail.

Phil was instructing his detail, including Gail, exactly how everything was to be placed in the cleared out magazine, once it had been identified as suspicious. Phil was prepared for more than twelve rounds to be placed in the suspect area. It had been determined that the initial screening would include all charges in question of being authentic.

After the training session, Gail, Phil and Fitzpatrick walked onto the flight deck.

"Senior," Fitzpatrick asked, "where will we disassemble the rounds after they are identified?"

"We," said Phil. "Will be Chief Cornell and I, everyone else will be clear of the flight deck, and the ship will be at General Quarters for a gas warfare drill. No one will be allowed topside during this period. We are taking on a portable x-ray device from the carrier while we are at sea, prior to entering Naples. Doc (the ships medical corpsman) will x-ray the charges that we have positively identified. When those are found, they will be replaced with known good ones. Those will come from ones we have in stock now. The bogus rounds will go in the hangar bay magazine."

Gail said, "The bad rounds will be set aside in Charleston and destroyed later. The shipment will continue as if all is normal, only with the charges we replace. This is another reason secrecy in what we are doing is paramount. Not even the ammo handlers in Charleston will know what is going on, as far as they know, it is just another load to be reworked."

Fitzpatrick asked, "What happens to the gas filled charges?"

Phil answered, "They will remain onboard until the operation is completed."

"Then, we'll be checking the magazines everyday like normal?" asked Fitz.

"Yes, the offload date will be driven by events yet to be disclosed. Are there any more questions?"

Gail spoke, "What happens if we have to open one or more charges to be one hundred percent sure of the contents?"

85

"I don't see that as happening because we will x ray the rounds, but if we do; I will be dressed in an NBC (Nuclear-Biological-Chemical) suit out on the fantail. If anything goes wrong, I can just dump the round over the side."

"Let's hope it doesn't come to that," said Fritz.

Gail and Phil returned to the Chiefs Mess to further discuss the upcoming operation.

"How is the transfer of ammo going to be accomplished?" asked Gail.

"We will be using our helicopters so we can keep positive control of the ammo. They will fly in to the airfield the day before we arrive at anchorage. That will clear the hangar for us to set up our scale and x ray equipment."

Gail said, "Sounds like you have it all under control, and by the way, you owe me a cup of coffee." With that, they entered the mess.

Chief Bagley was sitting at the table working on some reports that were due. He looked up when the two entered. "Hi you two, how's your day going so far?"

"Just about normal for a day at sea." said Gail jokingly.

Phil asked, "How about you shipmate?"

"About as well as can be expected I guess. Just hasn't been the same sense…, you know…, Robbie's death."

"I understand what you mean; I know you guys were close friends." Gail said, "It has been pretty rough on us too. This is something none of us will easily get over, if we ever do."

Bagley continued, "I can't understand why he was killed, it just doesn't make sense to me. The whole thing is senseless."

Phil said, "You are absolutely correct, it was senseless, and uncalled for. We will get to the bottom of it, trust me."

Gail looked at him with caution in her eyes, hoping he wouldn't say too much. Phil noticed the look he was getting from her.

"When I say we, I am referring to the US military and the justice system."

With that, she relaxed somewhat and handed Phil her empty cup. "Your turn," she said, trying to move the conversation forward.

Bagley smiled softly at them and said, "You two take care of each other, please; a good friend is so hard to lose, and can never be replaced." He gathered up his reports and headed off to the electronics office.

## CHAPTER 22

**A KNOCK CAME ON** the mess door. "Enter," said Phil. The door opened. It was Lt Pierce. "Got a moment Senior?"

"Always for my Division Officer, come in Lieutenant, what can I do for you?"

Pierce visually scanned the space to make sure they were all alone. "The Captain filled me in on the situation, along with the Weapons Officer." He said you and Agent Langston are heading up this situation and he wants us to support you anyway we can. What do you need from us?"

"I am happy to know you are in on this now; it makes me feel much better. *Chiefs Allen*/Langston, Cornell and I are happy to have support from you. It has been painful to keep this from you."

"I understand, Captain explained his position on all of this. Do you have everything set up for the on-load?"

"Yes sir, I believe we do. We can use some more help in the hangar when the ammo gets here. We have the scale to weigh each cage when it lands. We are looking at forty-eight rounds in each cage. Complete powder and shipping case, as you probably know already, weigh 43.5lbs each. That will be 2,088lbs plus 110lbs for the cage. There will be 11 cages, 10 full, one 41% filled"

"I'll be glad to help with that. Who will be looking for the markings and differences?"

Phil answered, "Chief Cornell here, and Petty Officer Fitzpatrick. We've had our training sessions already. I can go over everything with you in the Ordnance office where we can have some privacy."

"Sounds good Gunner, how about Langston, what is she going to be doing in this evolution?"

"Lying low, we're still trying to maintain animosity levels; it's tough though, because she's really a good person."

"I'll bet it is; let me know when you want to get together for that training. The Weapons Officer said, it's your show, he is there if you need him, but he has full confidence in you."

Phil responded, "Thank you, and again I'm glad you're in on this, I feel much better now."

"I'll see the two of you later." With that he turned and left the mess.

Phil turned to Gail, "This will make things more manageable at least. The Lt is a great guy, I'm relived the CO chose to include him."

"Let's go over this thing about opening the munitions again, I'm not sure I'm happy with it." She said.

"Trust me," he said. "It's not that big of a deal, I've done it before."

"And how long ago was that?" Gail quizzed.

Saturday afternoon the Boson's pipe broke the semi quietness of the soothing sound of water being pushed aside by the ship's hull as they churned their way slowly toward Naples. The Boson's Mate of the Watch announced, "Flight quarters, flight quarters, all hands man you're flight quarter stations."

The two CH-46 helicopters had been readied for flight the night before. Now they were prepped for launch. As they lifted off, the hangar was empty, and the wheels were in motion for the secretive mission set for the following day.

# CHAPTER 23

**A PORTION OF THE** crew was at breakfast, while preparations for entering port were in process throughout the ship. Crew members were cycling in and out of the mess areas, as work continued uninterrupted.

Moving slowly and accurately to the anchorage assigned to them, the Mt Mitchell's Conning Officer, Lt. Pierce, gave the order, "Let go the anchor."

The command was passed over the sound powered phones that connected the forecastle (fo'c'sle) and the bridge. On the fo'c'sle a seaman ready with a sledgehammer, struck the pelican hook that held the anchor chain in place. Suddenly the loud raucous sound of the anchor falling and the chain being pull out of the hawse pipe began. It ran unchecked and around the capstan, on the track known as the "wildcat".

As the anchor struck the bottom, the chain began to slow in its payout, now another seaman began to tighten the brake slowing the chain further, allowing him to control the payout. Enough chain is allowed to run and rest on the bottom; it is the chain that actually holds the ship in place, and not simply the anchor.

As the anchor struck bottom, the word was passed from the bridge, "Anchored, shift colors." The national ensign was now shifted back to the fantail flagstaff, and the quarterdeck watch set.

Back on the bridge the Captain praised Lt Pierce for a job well done. Then he said "I'm sure tomorrow will go well too."

"Yes sir Captain, my confidence level is very high." He was referring to the pending sarin gas hunt, not only the positioning and anchorage of the ship.

Monday morning, Phil was already in the hangar, where he had been most of the night. He had been preparing for the arrival of the ammo. Gail and Fitzpatrick joined him.

"Good morning Senior." Fitz said. "Good morning to the two of you, all ready for the challenge?"

"Yes, let's do this! Looks like you have been busy." Gail said.

"Good, glad you are, and yes I have." said Phil, "We are all set, all we need now is the ammo. This will be the staging area for initial inspection." Pointing to an area on the starboard side of the hangar, where he had set up metal pallets, with enough room to accommodate about thirty rounds of powder charges. He had marked the area with a quarantine placard.

"Over there is where we will place the suspect pieces. There's enough space for unknown rounds just in case there is any doubt in identifying some of them."

Fitz spoke up, "So the fork lift will set the cages at the hangar door, we will first weigh them then visually inspect and set aside any questionable ammo, am I correct in that?"

"Pretty much gunner," said Gail. "All of the charges will set here, in the hangar, overnight. This area is protected by a sprinkler system so we have coverage as far as that goes. But we will be here continuing to search and inspect, for as long as it takes."

Phil said, "The hangar and surrounding areas will be secured against any foot traffic until we have finished with our task. None of the cases will be opened until we are at sea. The next few days we will virtually be living in here. The rounds definitely identified will be placed in the magazine here in the hangar. It will be offloaded separately, when we get back to Charleston."

"Then, we will not actually open any of the rounds?" asked Fitz.

"Only if absolutely necessary," said Phil. "That will be the lucky devils at Yorktown."

"Better them than me; at least they are trained for this type of job." said Fitzpatrick.

"What time will the first load arrive?" asked Gail.

"About an hour from now, shortly after lunch, the choppers will bring only one pallet each at a time. This should provide plenty of time for us to weigh and visually inspect each and set aside any suspect rounds. I have a small handling party of Gunner's Mates and Fire Control techs to help. They all have secret clearances."

The word came from the airfield that the helos were on their way. Lt. Pierce had joined the group and was lending a hand with preparations.

Flight quarters were set, and the faint sound of rotary wings beating the air into submission was heard.

"Sounds like our H46's are here," Fitz said.

The first CH-46 hovered over the flight deck. The flight deck personnel directed the pilot to the spot above where the ammo was to be set. The pallet was set gently onto the deck, and the helo departed. The second bird had been standing off the port side waiting its turn. When the first bird cleared, the second one was waved in and directed where to place its load. Both helos were now outbound to fetch another load of charges.

The pallets were moved in with the electric fork lift and placed gently on the scale located inside the hangar bay. The weight was right on the money and set aside for visual inspection. The second pallet was processed with the same results. Nothing was found with the visual inspection.

Phil stated, "Two down and eight and a half to go." The next cycle of two pallets arrived with similar fanfare as the first. The pallets were brought in for weighing with the same results as the first. The weight on each of the first four pallets was 2,198lbs. Gail looked at Phil and Fitzpatrick with confidence still in their faces. Lt Pierce looked at everyone and just shrugged his shoulders. The third cycle of pallets was placed on the deck; the first pallet was moved in for weighing. The weight was right on speck.

While the second pallet was being moved in, Fitzpatrick noticed a small dent on the first one and then on another of the shipping containers. The weight was eight pounds light. "Set this one aside." He motioned to the forklift operator.

Roger and Gail started taking the pallet apart to set the questioned rounds aside.

"Look at this one." Roger said. "The wire is twisted counter clockwise. Gail motioned for Phil to come look.

"Looks like you guys struck pay dirt. Let's hope our luck holds out."

As good luck does at times occur, so it did on this day. Twelve powder cases were found that showed physical signs of tampering. No x-ray and no dismantling had to be done. However, the easy part was done.

The gas had been recovered and accounted for. At least these vials would not be used to harm anyone. Phil made sure the charges containing the sarin gas vials were securely placed in the magazine in the hangar bay. The remainders of rounds were moved via elevator, to a magazine below decks, for the duration of the cruise.

Lt. Pierce reported to the Captain that the mission had been accomplished; all bogus rounds accounted for, and all ammo was safely and securely stowed in the proper magazines. Worrell expressed his gratitude, and asked Pierce to pass along a hearty well done to Phil and his crew.

# CHAPTER 24

**BACK IN THE CHIEFS** mess, Phil sat quietly sipping a cup of freshly brewed tea, while Gail enjoyed a glass of lemon iced tea. She looked at Phil and asked, "Do you think anything will get back to normal anytime in the future?"

"I think the terrorist have defined a new normal for us. I know we've got to try to keep things on a normal footing; but I'm thinking things will never be the old normal, or that we have come to regard as being normal. We have two days left in Naples. What do you say we hop a train and go down the coast to Pompeii?"

"What brought that on?" Gail asked.

"I just want to be alone with you for a while, you know, get away from all of this."

"That sounds like an offer I can't refuse." She said, in her best Mafioso voice.

Phil managed a faint chuckle, "Don't even go there. I've had enough drama for a while." With that the two went into their respective berthing quarters to change into civilian attire, and make the boat ride ashore.

Once on the landing, they headed for Boston Blackie's, a

popular hangout for the fleet. While on their way they stopped to admire Castle Nuovo (New Castle in Italian).

Gail said, "I did read up a bit on some of the sights around here, and the building of this famous castle was started in the year 1279. Since then, it has been renovated and expanded many times; and by the way, a burial site was discovered under the castle too! Spooky."

"My dear, you are a most interesting lady." They moved on to Blackie's where they encountered a few of the crew enjoying the local fare. After a refreshing gin and tonic each, they continued the stroll east on Corso Umberto I, and on to Piazza Garibaldi and the train station. Phil purchased two tickets for Pompeii and they were on the way.

"I thought we would see Agent Love here, but I guess he couldn't make it. He did say he would meet us here."

"You don't suppose anything bad has happened to him do you?" Gail asked.

"I think he's fine, probably went looking for Langston that would be my guess."

"Speaking of Sam, I haven't seen her in the past couple of days."

"You're right *Linda* Gail," said Phil, "You haven't been able to play matchmaker in a day or two, have you?"

She promptly popped him on the shoulder then gave him a kiss on the cheek. "I just think they are right for each other."

"Yeah, well I think you may have something there."

The two enjoyed the day touring through the excavations of Pompeii and the surrounding area. That evening they dined at a quaint little restaurant, and enjoyed a simple meal of pizza and wine. The train ride back to Naples was cool and quiet. They were alone in the back of the rear car. Press together in the seat they kissed and snuggled in close to keep each other warm against the cool Mediterranean air.

Suddenly the door separating the cars opened and a Middle Eastern man sat down in the front seat. He was facing away from them and seemed to be fixated on the passing landscape. But Phil noticed he was actually using the window as a quasi-mirror, all the while glancing back at them. Gail was leaning into Phil's warm body when he squeezed her gently.

"Do not react, but I think we are being followed." He said quietly.

She slowly opened her eyes and said, "The man in the picture, the waiter in training."

"Yes, Mohamed Masawi. I don't think he knows that we have seen a picture of him, or that we can identify him. We never crossed paths in the hotel or restaurant."

"Yeah, but he knows who we are." The next fifteen minutes back to Naples seemed like an eternity, but finally the train pulled into the busy station at Garibaldi.

They departed the train trying not to look spooked, but knowing that this guy had killed two people in cold blood, was a frightening concept. By deciding to hire a cab back to the dock instead of walking, they hoped to get clear of this murderer.

Each of them looked over their shoulder as the cab pulled away from the station. No one there; how long had he followed them? Had he been trailing them all day?

A more secure feeling came over them as the cab pulled into the parking area at the head of the pier, there stood two armed Carabinieri officers. The Carabinieri is the senior of the two Italian police forces; closer to the army than the regular Polizia or State Police.

Phil paid the cabbie and smiled at the two officers who simply nodded their heads in return.

"That was to close for comfort," said Gail. "Let's ask the beach guard if they have seen Sam, I mean Chief Allen. We need to know if she and Love are ok."

The couple approached the ship's beach guard.

"Hi Senior Chief, Chief, how are the two of you tonight?"

"Great," said Phil. "Have you seen Chief Allen tonight?"

"Funny thing you ask," the beach guard quipped. "She and that NIS guy left a note for you..., let's see, here it is... they left this about two hours ago; said they were going into the city for the night."

"Thanks," Phil said. He and Gail moved away to read the note. He opened the sealed note: *"Waiter is in town, meet us at the Seaman's Club, getting a room there."* It was signed Jim.

"I guess we know they are ok," said Gail.

"Yes, that is a relief, but what else is up?" Phil asked not expecting an answer. "Well, it's off to the Seaman's Club. We'll find out when we get there. I hope that cab is still there, it's a short walk to the club, just past the castle and up the hill, but with Mohamed in town, the cab is safer."

"Have you been here before? Naples,... you seem to know where things are located; Boston Blackie's, the train station, and now the Seaman's Club."

Phil smiled and said "After Vietnam, 1970, I was stationed on the USS Julius A. Furer, FFG6. I had taken some time off, reenlisted and was sent to the East Coast. The ship was home ported out of Newport, Rhode Island, and on a Med-Cruise. After that tour I went back west, my daughter was born while I was gone. Susan stayed with her mother while I was deployed. She didn't want to move across country and that far away from her mom. My mother-in-law and I had a disagreement that lasted fourteen years. It finally ended on the day after Susan and I were divorced..., so yes, I am a little familiar with a few places in the Med."

"One day *Mac*, you will have to sit down and tell me all your little secrets."

"We have time; I don't plan on letting you get out of my sight any time soon." He said, as he motioned to the taxi driver who was still there, talking with the two Carabinieri Officers. "Where to?" The driver asked.

"The Seaman's Club," Phil answered.

# CHAPTER 25

**IN AN EARTHEN BRICK** hut somewhere in Beirut, Lebanon's Baalbek sector, located in the Beqaa Valley, a messenger delivered a note to Imad Mughniyah, leader of the Islamic Jihad. He took the message, opened it and smiled. The gift has been delivered and the party is set. This brought an even bigger smile to his face, "Our brothers have succeeded in our quest, soon the infidel will be stricken with fear again in his own house!" Cheers went up all around the brick hut, as gunfire erupted in celebration of their triumph, cries of Allahu Akbar (God is Great) was shouted again and again.

Although the terrorists knew another six months would go by before the sarin gas would reach the US, they were prepared to wait. The feeling was that they had to eternity to convert the world to Islam.

Besides, they had more plans for disruption and killing in the name of Allah.

Phil paid the cabbie once again. "Would you like for me to wait for you, the driver asked?" "Not necessary," Phil said. "I think we'll be here a while this time."

"Here is my card in case; the man at the desk can call." The driver offered his card to Gail. She took the card and thanked him.

While climbing the stairs, Gail said, "This reminds me of an old Bogart movie, this place is…,"

"Rustic?" Phil said.

"No spooky." She quipped.

"It has been around a long time," Phil said. "You know wooden ships…."

They reached the top of the staircase and he pushed the door open slowly. The two of them looked around, not seeing Sam and Jim at first.

"Over there," said Gail, "In the back corner." They proceeded across the large almost vacant room to join Langston and Love.

"God it's good to see you two," Gail said while reaching out with a hug for the two of them.

"Where have you been hiding Sam?"

"With Jim," she answered.

Gail stymied for a moment said, "With Jim?"

Not the way you're thinking, we've been laying low. We are trying to avoid being detected by the terrorist; word from *central* is, as we put in the note we left with the beach guard, the *waiter* is in town."

Phil said, "We know, he followed us to Pompeii and back today."

Jim Love said, "What? He followed you all day?"

"We think it was all day, although we didn't see him until our return trip. We were in the rear train car alone, and then he walked in and sat down at the front of the car just as calm and normal as could be. He sat with his back to us but kept looking at the reflection of us in the glass. At first we thought he was staring out of the window; then Gail noticed that he had turned to an angle where he could keep an eye on us."

"Do you think he knows that you knew who he was?" Sam asked.

"I don't think so, we continued to act as if nothing happened, including laughing and joking somewhat." Gail said.

"Let's hope so," said Jim. "We don't want to give anything away."

"Speaking of giving anything away, do you suppose we could get anything to eat and drink around here?" Gail asked. "I'm famished."

Sam laughed and said, "You aren't pregnant are you?"

The question completely threw her for a loop. "I don't think so." She said as she looked at Phil. Phil's face had turned red as Sam and Jim were laughing at his reaction. Gail started laughing too, "You should see the look on your face right now, priceless! Of course I'm not pregnant; I am a little smarter than that, Philip. But I had you going for a moment."

Jim was motioning for the waiter to come over when Gail asked. "Are you guys going back to the ship tonight?"

"Jim and I have a room for the night; I should say, rooms for the night; for your edification Gail. We have one on temporary reserve for you two if you want to stay; it's just down the hall from ours. Safety in numbers kind a thing you know."

"I think we will take that option after the day we've had. *Our waiter*, not the one here, probably thinks we returned to the ship for the night." Phil said.

"Let's start with oysters on the half shell and manicotti," suggested Sam, "and a bottle of white wine."

"My word, someone is ambitious," said Gail, "You like oysters don't you Jim?"

It was now Jims turn to have the red face, as the ubiquitous laughter was directed his way.

"Ok, ok, the joke is on me this time, but at least I'm with friends."

Sam smiled softly at Jim and said, "Yes you are, my little red faced friend, you're certainly among friends." With that she pinched his cheek, which made him blush even more.

"What did I do to deserve all this love?" he asked. "Get it? L-O-V-E!"

"Sam laughed out loud and said, "I'm the one that's supposed to say that." Then she caught herself, "Oops." She put her hand to her mouth and looked at Gail, who, by this time was in tears with laughter.

Phil said, "We haven't had any wine yet; and you are all giddy; although it is good to be able to laugh at ourselves, even in the face of adversity. I guess this makes us normal," As he looked at Gail with laughter on his face.

After the food was gone and the wine finished, the quartet of friends headed off to their respective rooms.

About thirty minutes after they had all supposedly settled into their rooms Gail heard a sound in the hallway. She peered through the peep hole in the room door, thinking it could be Masawi. What she saw relieved her.

She turned her back to the door and a smile came to her face. It was Jim, in the hallway outside of Sam's room. She turned back and peered again through the opening, only to see Jim slip quietly into Sam's room. The door closed slowly and softly behind him. She whispered in a subdued voice, "Good night you two."

Phil asked "Is there a problem out there?"

"No; just the oysters catching up with someone; now come here lover, we have some catching up to do too."

## CHAPTER 26

**THE NEXT MORNING AT** breakfast, Phil and Gail were the first ones to show. They ordered coffee and talked for a while. Gail didn't mention to him that she had observed Jim going into Sam's room the previous evening. She decided it would be better if she maintained plausible deniability at this point. Instead, she would wait for Samantha to broach the subject sometime in the future.

Fifteen minutes or so had passed when the other two came in and joined them for breakfast.

"Well, how did you sleep last night Sam?" asked Gail.

"Really good, best rest I've had in quite a while."

Gail continued, "How about you Jim, how did you sleep?"

"Like a baby, that mattress is fantastic."

"Wonderful, I'm glad." She smiled at Sam who was, at this time engrossed in the menu, but she glanced up to see Gail's expression. Samantha being the good FBI agent she was, remained expressionless.

Gail could not stop, and leave it alone though, "Did you guys hear anything in the hallway last night, about thirty minutes after we locked in?"

There was a moment of silence then Jim spoke, "Yes, I think it was room service next door to me." Samantha maintained her focus on the menu.

"I'm sure it was." Said Gail, "I'm sure it was."

Sam looked up at Gail and asked, "So what's for breakfast?"

"Ham and eggs," responded Gail, "ham and eggs."

"What is on our agenda for today?" asked Phil.

Jim answered quickly. "A little sightseeing and then a brief lunch then we have an appointment with my boss at Sixth Fleet, HQ. I think he is going to assign me to follow you through the remainder of the deployment; back-up for you Sam, and safety for you two."

"Sixth Fleet, that's in Gaeta, so shouldn't we skip sightseeing and lunch, we may be seen together out sightseeing; besides that's a long drive up the coast from here." Phil said.

"We're not driving," stated Jim. "We're flying by helicopter, one of your CH-46s; they will take us up and back, and the *waiter* has moved on to Athens, to stay ahead of the cargo; all this is according to my contact at *central*."

"What is the purpose of this meeting?" asked Sam.

"I think that is supposed to be disclosed in the meeting. I wasn't given any other info, just to be there with you three."

Sam said, "This is getting more and more like a crime novel, and I'm not sure I like where this is headed, but I'm along for the ride. When I first took this assignment it was just a plain undercover operation; now it's turned into an international terror plot. Where will it end?"

Gail said, "I guess if we knew that, Allen, we could just go there and wait for it."

Samantha looked at Gail and said, "Stuff it Blondie."

Gail and Phil started chuckling, but Jim failed to understand the moment. He was sitting with a puzzled look on his face.

Phil said, "Jim, you just had to be in this from the beginning."

"I guess so. You took that very well Gail, I thought that was an insult, and coming from such a nice person."

Gail responded with, "It is a term of endearment between us; Sam can explain more in detail tonight." With that she turned to Samantha, "Can't you Sam?"

Sam looked at Jim and stated, "You Bet'cha I can, and I'm not from Minnesota."

With that said, Jim shook his head back and forth, "What strange friends I have chosen." He expressed.

"And you better not forget it," laughed Sam. "Let's get out of here before this conversation gets out of control."

"You mean it hasn't already?" asked Jim.

Departing the restaurant Sam slid her hand into Loves. Gail nudged Phil in the side and pointed this out.

He just smiled at her and said, "Happy camper now?" She caressed his arm and said, "You Bet'cha!"

## CHAPTER 27

**THE TIME HAD COME** for the trip to Gaeta, Italy just up the coast from Naples. The four made their way back to the ship where they would board the helo for the transit to Gaeta. As they were awaiting the helo to arrive the Executive officer approached them.

"Senior Chief, I have something for you to take with you."

"Yes sir, May I ask what it is, and who does it go to?"

The XO handed him a sealed envelope. "This is not to be opened until your meeting; it is to stay in your possession until you reach Sixth Fleet Headquarters. You will hand it Chief of Staff, he will open it in front of the four of you, is that understood?"

"Yes Sir XO, certainly is, but no hint?"

"I think you all are in for a surprise…, and from the Captain, 'Watch your six', and might I add, ditto, happy hunting."

The helicopter was now inbound. With that the XO shook all their hands and turned and walked away. The quartet of investigators stood looking puzzled over the scene that had just taken place.

Jim said, "I told you I didn't know everything that was going on; just enough to keep me in the outer loop."

They boarded the helo and started their way to Gaeta. The four of them were now in a quandary as to what the meeting was to reveal. In flight each of them couldn't help but focusing on the mysterious envelope, and its last minute delivery; but most of all what it contained. Furthermore, what did this package hold for their future?

---

The flight lasted about thirty five minutes and was now approaching the helo pad at Sixth Fleet HQ. Jim was the first to depart the aircraft, followed by Sam, Gail then Phil, tightly clutching the envelope handed to him by his XO little more than a half an hour ago.

They were met at the edge of the helo pad by a Lieutenant Commander and were escorted to the staff conference room for the meeting. As they entered the building, bewilderment still was with them. Soon they would all know what the future had in store for them.

Entering the room, Jim noticed his boss, Agent Martin Nitti, standing at the map of the Middle East.

"Martin," he called, "Good to see you, how long have you been here?"

Martin turned and smiled at Jim, "Good to see you James, I came in yesterday. Introduce me to the rest of the group."

James started with Sam, "This is FBI Agent Samantha Langston, Chief Petty Officer Gail Cornell, and Senior Chief Petty Officer Philip Mattingly."

"It's really good to finally put real faces with the names. James has told me a lot of good things about all of you, is any of it true?" He was chuckling and taking time to shake each of their hands when Sam spoke. "I think he can tell a tall tale when needed, but hopefully not in this case."

"Yes Agent Langston, I am finally glad to meet you. Your Captain Worrell speaks very highly of your talents, keep an eye on James, he can be a handful at times." He chuckled and moved to Gail, Chief Cornell, it is a pleasure to meet you. You are the one that introduced the Senior Chief to all this, correct?"

"Yes sir, I am to blame." Then he moved to Phil, "Finally, Philip Mattingly; Senior Chief Gunner's Mate. Old Navy man myself, got out after Vietnam, river boats, GMG3. One tour, one enlistment, went into law enforcement, and well here we are."

"Glad to meet you sir." Phil said.

"I understand that you have a little more experience than normal, for your rating."

"In some ways, yes sir" said Phil "Others, not so much."

"A man of humility James, just what we like in a man."

"Yes boss, I haven't heard him brag once, about any of his past accomplishments with the CIA."

Gail looked at Phil and said softly, "We've got to have a long talk mister."

The Chief Staff Officer entered the room and everyone snapped to attention. "Cary on" he said, "Please everyone have a seat. This will not take long. Senior I believe you have something for me?"

"Yes sir I do." Phil handed the envelope across the heavy mahogany table. The CSO wasted no time in opening and removing the contents.

"What we have here folks is a new set of orders for each of you temporarily assigning all of you to work under the direction and auspices of the Central Intelligence Agency of The United States of America. You have been directed to come here for a short indoctrination into what your mission will entail; morphing from what it was, to what is to be. And for God's sake I hope someone up the chain knows what they are getting you into. Personally I want to strike hard and…, well that's enough of what I want. A person whom will remain unknown to you by name, but will simply be coded, 'Timekeeper', will be your contact from this moment on. You will not have any contact with your deployed unit until further notice. Your personal belongings are at this moment being packed up and will be stored here, at Sixth Fleet, until such time as you may need them again. Chief Cornell, you will be primarily responsible for all communications between this team and Timekeeper. Although any of you may contact him if needed. You will also, oversee all finances of the team, we have to take advantage of your training somewhere in all this to justify your participation, and I do mean that, you are a vital part of the mission. Mattingly you have proven yourself in the past; I know, if you have to, you can do the job required."

The CSO looked at Phil across the top of his reading glasses. Phil nodded his head in silent understanding.

"As for you two," looking at Sam and Jim, you will without doubt, have to always be the eyes and ears of the team, your agencies training will hold you in good stead. Any questions you have, please direct them to your contact, he will join you shortly after I leave. I wish you the best, watch your six." With that, he left the conference room. They all looked at each other in stunned silence; at what had just happened.

"I've seen this show before, we're in for a treat," Phil stated.

The door opened, and in walked a well-built man in his mid-thirties carrying a black nylon bag.

"Good afternoon, I am Timekeeper, and I will be your contact from this moment on. I'm sure you have questions. Gail raised her hand and asked, "What the hell is going on here?"

"Let me see you are Gail Cornell, right? I was informed you would ask the first question, good for you, and you don't have to raise your hands. What is going on is a covert, outside the normal agency box; an effort, to capture Masawi, better known to you as, 'the waiter'. Also I understand that you are all volunteers, so that make things easier."

"How did WE volunteer?" asked Gail?

"After your friend was killed and the college student murdered, you were in too deeply not to volunteer, are you wanting out?"

Gail glanced at Phil; he raised his eyebrows, as if to say now is your chance. "Hell no, I'm in for the duration."

"Great! Anyone else?"

Phil asked, "What is our cover, and mode of operation?"

"Good question, you will carry on as you have been, pretend tourist, only this time we want you to take him out of the operation, any way you can. The agency will not be involved directly; you will be on your own for the most part. We will be following and keeping updates. If for any reason you are compromised, you are acting on your own, you know, with vengeance for your friend's murder."

"The orders removing you from the ship simply stated that you all were too close to the event, and were removed for your own safety and wellbeing. Your assistant agents, Langston have been informed, and will remain on the ship. You can call on them if they are needed, but try to keep this to the four of you if at all possible. The bureau is aware of all. By the way, they will be presented with commendations on all their actions thus far. Now with that said, here are your passports, rental car, tourist maps, and in the other bag."

Timekeeper knocked on the wall and a man entered with a second bag and placed on the table. "These are your weapons to be used in the op. Any weapons you have on you, or in your possession, at this time are to be surrendered to me, and will be reissued to you, at the successful conclusion to this operation; even if you're not supposed to have one, Philip."

He slowly reached below the table and removed a small Walther PPK from his ankle holster and placed it gently on the table in front of Timekeeper. Gail again surprised by Phil had nothing to say. Jim and Sam slid their weapons across the table reluctantly. At that point Timekeeper produced the weapons to be used on the operation.

"Only to protect your lives, may I present to you the Russian made Makarov PM, it weighs only 26oz and is a 9mm semi auto double/single action pistol. It operates the same as the weapons you are used to using, and uses the 9mm Parabellum round. If you need training at this point, all is lost. I know this is not the case though, silly me." He chuckled at his own remark.

"How are we to communicate, when necessary?" Sam asked.

"In your bag of tricks here, pointing to the bag he had brought in, you will find a credit type card, pick up any pay phone, and simply punch in the number printed on it. Do not go through an operator, it will automatically connect you with my center and directly to me if need be. My center is manned twenty four hours a day, seven days a week. Any one there can help you if you get in a jam, but I will always be notified in any case. In the bag you will also find two sets of keys to the vehicle parked outside, this will be your transportation for the op. Also you have real credit cards in your names, but the bill will go to my center as well. So keep it real. Your assignment is to find and capture, alive if possible, Mohamed Masawi. Your basic itinerary is the same as the ship. Be ahead of it at each port and establish contact with me and set up your base of operation. There are other things in the bag, become familiar with them, Mattingly, you probably have seen these items before, you can explain to the others. That is all I have, be mindful of your situations and happy hunting." With that he turned and marched out of the room.

Jim turned to Martin and said, "What advice do you have boss?"

"This Masawi character is a snake, you only get one chance in a gunfight, make it count." He rose from his seat and was exiting the room; he stopped and turned, "And,… watch your six for God sake."

As the door closed behind him Sam said, "We've been hearing that phrase a lot lately."

Gail said to Phil, "Your turn, you've been awfully quiet today mister."

"I hoped it would never get this far. But it has, so let's get started by getting in the car and finding a place to set up for the night."

"Good place to start," said Sam. "I'm starving."

"You aren't pregnant, are you?" Gail asked.

"I'm smarter than that too," she answered. Jim, red faced but smiling, picked up his new weapon and headed for the door. "My friends," he said, as he reached for the door.

Phil, shaking his head again said, "My world and welcome to it." They all gathered their new gear and went in search of the car.

# CHAPTER 28

**THE QUARTET REACHED THE** rental car, Jim said, "This is the way to travel, a 1983 Mercedes 300sd." He stopped abruptly, "Why do I, all of a sudden feel like a man that could be headed in the direction of his last meal?"

"Get over it, we have many more before the last one," Sam interjected, "Phil drives first," she continued, "He's been here before, and I mean that in more ways than just, geographically."

He pulled a set of the keys from his pocket and held them up, "Glad to oblige. I know where there is a perfect hotel with a great view, and dynamite restaurant."

"Please don't say dynamite," said Gail. The other two chimed in with agreement.

"I'll be more selective with my choice of words from here forward." He moved into the driver's seat.

Heading out from the Sixth Fleet compound, now in their *almost new* Mercedes, Phil said, "We are topped off with fuel too. I suppose they didn't want us to stop for a while, shall we head in the direction of Athens?"

"That's going to be a long drive, about six-hundred miles I believe," said Gail.

Phil glanced over to and said, "Really, we aren't driving all the way to Athens my dear."

She thought for a moment then said, "Then there must be a ferry if we plan on taking the car."

"Bingo! Give the little lady a kewpie doll."

She reached over and punched him on the shoulder, "Don't be a butt, it's unbecoming to you."

"Careful," he said, "I have witnesses that you struck a senior."

She looked over her left shoulder and said, "You guys look out the window for a while, I'm going to kill him." Jim and Sam were snickering at the two of them.

"You two remind me of my mom and dad, they were always picking at one another," Sam said teasingly, "they have been married for almost forty years now."

Gail cut a quick glance at Phil, "Don't get any ideas," she said.

"What? I'm just driving the car." This team was on the road to becoming lifelong friends, not just on the road to Athens.

"I figure we can make Brindisi on the East Coast by eighteen-thirty; and then make the nineteen-thirty ferry to Patras, Greece. That will give us overnight to rest and refresh. We should arrive in Greece tomorrow about thirteen hundred or so. From there it's just a short hour or so down the coast road to Athens, where we can set up our op-center."

"He never ceases to amaze me," Gail said, "About the time I think I'm figuring him out, bam, he comes up with some more off-the-wall stuff."

"No," he said, "I read about it, I had planned to take a trip there, and I did my research, I have a good memory you know."

"I have a good memory too," said Sam, "You were going to fill us in on the items in the bag, can you do that and drive?"

"My god," Phil said, "Now she's on my case, what is this, pick on Philip day?" Everyone was enjoying a chuckle on Phil this time; then he started explaining the contents.

"First we have the pictures of him, and his known accomplices. Then there will be detail maps of all the areas we are expected to cover in our search for him. A compact camera for travel pictures i.e. surveillance. Cash, about twenty thousand, broken up into all the local currencies, for each region on the map I covered before. Then there are restraints, to secure an individual: if he/she," he glanced at Gail, "should get out of control. Now there is the matter of the syringes. Is anyone afraid to give an injection to our creep if need be?" This was answered by a "no" from everyone.

"Good," he said. "That brings me to the next item. There is a cyanide tablet in a small metal tube, not for us, but for our guest if he gets totally out of control. The shot will put him to sleep for about eight hours, so we have to move quickly once we have him subdued. This car has a hidden compartment about his size under the rear seat. That will be for his first class travel arrangement. Oh yes, a couple of really sharp flat throwing knives for, whatever. Anything else we will have to learn together."

"Sounds as if the forces that be, are trying to turn us into impromptu assassins," Said Jim.

"It could turn out that way if we don't watch what we do carefully," Phil stated. "We don't have to terminate him, in fact I would prefer not to. We will get more millage out of capturing him right off their own little playground."

They continued the drive to Italy's southeastern coast. The Adriatic and Ionian Seas meet, just below the Port of Brindisi; the bristling seaside city where they would board the ferry to Greece.

Each member of this ad hoc team had turned inward to their own thoughts and concerns. Now was the time for reflection, not after the action starts. Each seemed to be preparing in their individual way. Phil, the others thought; apparently had all this figured out. But, he was thinking just how badly things could get.

Arriving in Brindisi, and on time, seemed to settle the others down somewhat. They began to feel more in charge of their emotions; and as though this would be nothing more than another ordinary kidnapping, and smuggling the bad guy out of a foreign country without getting caught case, simple. The team had unconsciously begun to get primed for whatever came at them.

Arriving at the port, Phil parked the sedan. "I'll get the tickets if you guys watch my back, it should take just a minute or so."

They agreed and he went after the ferry ticket to Patras. While Phil was busy with the cashier, the others officially elected him, the pseudo leader of the team; after all he had worked with the CIA before. This was something none of the others had done, and he seemed to know his way around quite well. With that settled they continued to watch out for anything out of the ordinary.

Phil was on his way to the car brandishing four fresh tickets for the ferry, when Gail noticed a folded note protruding from his shirt pocket.

As he slipped into the driver's seat, Gail said, "Guess what? You've been elected as head of this team, which deserves a cheek kiss."

As she pulled him toward her side of the car, she snatched the note from his pocket, flipped it over the seat into the Jim's lap. "What does it say Jim," asked Gail.

Both Jim and Sam read the note. - Ferry tickets waiting, Brindisi for tonight – arrive Patras tomorrow afternoon – take coast road south to destination. Contact after set up -. "Gail, you must read this," Jim said.

Gail read the note. She took the note and read it. "You sneaky bag of bones, I'll fix you, you just wait. Phil, when did you get the note?" Sam asked.

"It was in the bag. I knew the launch instructions are always in there, part of the deal for us rookies. That will be our last bit of advice though. I thought I'd have fun with it. I left the thing sticking out of my pocket as we left the conference room; I thought someone would notice sooner, and call me on it. Still want me as team leader?"

"Hell yes," said Jim, "That was a good one, and anyone that cagy, needs to be out front."

"The way I see that," said Phil. "This thing is split four ways, but if everything goes wrong, I'll be in charge and take the responsibility, ok?"

"Sam, what do you think?" asked Gail.

"The way I look at it is, we're in this crap together, and we may as well share the paper." She continued. "After any discussion, and if we need a tie breaker, Phil should be it."

Phil shared with them, "I believe everyone will do whatever needs to be done, to pull this thing off. Just remember, there is always danger; but that doesn't mean, that you can't share some laughter at the right times. This is the simple point that I wanted to make. I just wanted to pass it on to you, as it was passed to me. This little spoof helped to lighten the mood for all of us, and that's a good thing."

The ferry's loadmaster waved them up. The Mercedes was the next to load. Phil pulled the car slowly into the designated space, slipped it into park, locked the emergency brake and shut the ignition off. "Now it's time for a glass of *Chateau de white grape*, care to join me?"

"I don't remember that being on your list," said Gail.

"I said that note was the last instruction from them, we're on our own now."

"I don't know," Sam said. "We may want to put it to a vote, how many say yes?" Everyone but Phil raised their hand.

Jim said chuckling "Is it ok if I have some of the *Chateau de red grape?*"

"Well, as de facto leader of the pack, I have to vote yes, it's specialty of the houseboat, motion carried your turn to buy Gail." With that he exited the vehicle followed by the others who were giggling and laughing like there was no tomorrow. Phil's little prank had brought them closer, and that was his goal all along.

# CHAPTER 29

**AFTER RETRIEVING A GLASS** of wine each, the quasi tourist, found their way to the upper deck. There they would be able to observe the exquisite beauty of the surrounding area.

"This scenic view makes a person almost want to forget all the troubles in the world, doesn't it Phil?" He looked back at Jim and said, "Almost my friend, almost."

Jim asked, "How are we going to capture this guy alive, and transport him out of Greece? If we can catch him here, that is."

"We will get with the ladies and hash this out but I think if we can continue what Robinson started, we will be able to flush him out. Only thing is, this time we will have to lure him out of the public eye, and somewhere we have concealment. We'll have to take him down with force; all of us will have to take part in the take down."

"There is a good sized Lebanese community in Athens," said Jim. "Many expatriates are moving there. If we can find a common meeting area where we might be able to set up an observation point…,"

Phil interrupted, "Or let it be known who we are, and that way possibly attracting our subject to us."

"That is a mighty dangerous plan with this animal; he'd likely be akin to a, cornered, *pissed off badger.*"

"You are absolutely correct in your analogy, but even a badger can be cornered and overwhelmed by a pack of good dogs, especially four, armed dogs."

"We better run this by the other half of the team," said Jim.

"Flip for it?" Phil said.

"No, team leader, that's your job." Sam and Gail were standing at the railing, enjoying their glasses of wine when the men sidled up on each side them.

"This looks ominous," said Sam, "I think these two have cooked up something that we're not going to like very well."

"Give him a chance," Jim volunteered.

Phil looked at him, "Thanks partner, toss me on that track alone." Jim chuckled, and Phil started explaining the basic idea of the blueprint for capturing Masawi.

Sam suggested, "The key to something like this, will be selecting the right location. One that will allow us to whisk him out without being blatant about it; and to be able to pull it off; without getting killed, I like it."

Gail chimed in, "Access to an alley where we can quickly move the car into, stuff him in the trunk and speed away."

Phil, Jim and Sam looked at her speechless.

Sam broke the silence, "It will be a good idea to neutralize him in some way first darling, and then we can transfer him quietly out a rear entrance. We will want to draw as little attention to the capture as possible. Some likely locations will have to be scouted out once we get settled in Athens. This will give us about two days to prepare. For now though, let's check on our sleeping arrangements and get some dinner."

Jim said, "Great idea! I need another wine and some food, after all this planning, I'm famished."

Phil asked, "You're not pregnant are you?" With that question, they all laughed shook their heads, and headed for the cozy little bistro onboard the ferry.

Taking their seats, they browsed the double sided, single sheet menu. Gail ordered caprese salad, Phil a cheese Stromboli, Sam the Greek salad, and Jim splurged by ordering the chicken parmesan, and of course the glass of red wine. They agreed to refrain from discussing the op, until they could find a more secure spot. Probably that would be in the Mercedes, on the way to Athens.

Gail, at the behest of Phil, went to the small office where she was to acquire the keys to the small sleeping rooms that had been reserved for them by Timekeeper. She returned with two keys.

Sam looked at her and asked. "I guess it's you and I tonight, right Gail?"

Gail tossed the key to her and said. "I have my key, and roommate. See you guys in about eight hours."

With that she took Phil by the hand and marched him off in the general direction of the berthing area.

Sam turned her head toward Jim. "Where are you going to sleep tonight?"

"Outside your room I guess, or maybe right here, if the bar stays open all night," he said with a wide grin on his face.

"I can't let you do that," she said. "I guess I'll have to tend to you tonight little boy." She took him by his right arm and led him away to the tiny room with a double size bed. "I want you to behave yourself tonight," she said.

"Just like night before last?" he asked. Samantha turned to him, "Exactly like that," she said, as she moved in and placed a kiss on his lips. "Exactly," she repeated.

# CHAPTER 30

**THE NEXT MORNING THE** ferry was still approximately eight hours from Patras. Passengers began emerging from compartments all over the ship. A few had slept in chairs and on benches, others in their cars or caravans they had driven onboard. Sam and Jim had awakened early and retrieved coffee and pastries from the breakfast bar located in the bistro.

Standing at the railing together, Jim had his arm around her, and hers was tightly around his waist. She was looking into his eyes and smiling when Gail walked onto the deck behind them.

"Hello there you two," she said. "Had breakfast yet?"

They quickly dropped their embrace. "We had coffee, and some really delicious pastry from the breakfast bar," answered Sam. "The coffee is fresh too," said Jim.

Gail with a wide smile on her face said, "Bet the pastry wasn't as sweet as the sight I just saw."

"Just won't give up will you?" said Sam. "Well get over it, you're going to see more of it, right Jim?"

He looked at Gail and said, "The FBI lady is right. She said if I agree with her all day today, she wouldn't cuff me to the door knob tonight." Sam slapped him on his shoulder and said, "Be nice now, I fed you this morning."

"Oh goodness, you'll never get rid of him now." Gail said. "But it is nice to see you're getting along so well.

"I felt sorry for him couldn't let him sleep outside last night," Sam said.

"Lucky for me, "said Jim. About that time Phil came out of the bistro with a coffee in his hand.

"I thought you were going to sleep all day," said Gail.

"Wanted to," he said. "I didn't get to sleep till after midnight. The newlyweds next to us were busy most of the evening."

Gail said, "Don't be silly, these two were next to us last night." Gail turned to Sam for a reaction.

"Must have been the handcuffs on the doorknob," she said. Phil raised his eyebrows while the other three were chuckling.

The four of them spent the next few hours walking around the decks, talking, and enjoying the scenery of Greece's West Coast. The hours passed quickly. It was time to get back to business.

Jim was driving, and as he pulled the Mercedes into the traffic, he made a left turn and headed eastward down the coastal highway E94 toward Rio. The team would follow this highway down the coast of Peloponnese, while overlooking the waters of the Gulf of Corinth; finally to the city of Corinth. From there, they would travel north east, and on to Athens.

"How long is the drive to Athens from here?" asked Sam.

Phil said, "About three hours, give or take. The road can be dangerous in places, so we have to move along cautiously."

"Yeah Jim, keep your mind on the road," said Sam. Jim looked into the rear view mirror, Gail was listening to what Sam was saying, but Phil seemed to be in deep thought.

"What are you thinking about so deeply?" asked Jim. "Is my driving scaring you?"

125

"No, No, you're doing fine. Just thinking about where the ship will be anchored. That would be a great place to keep a terrorist once he is subdued. He could even be flown off in one of our helos."

"You mean like the one that kidnapped us; I like what you're saying," Sam affirmed.

"I think the captain would go for that, he'd love to host this guy aboard for a day or so, you know, ham and eggs for breakfast, ham and cheese sandwich for lunch and pork ribs for dinner."

"Ouch!" said Gail, "That's tough, bad for the blood pressure you know." That was her way of agreeing with Sam.

"Another thing," said Phil. "There is an American style restaurant in Glyfada, south of Athens proper, it's called *Big Burger*."

"What else but?" said Gail.

"Really," said Phil. "This guy probably won't hang out in a Muslim joint; he will go where the Americans go, that will be *Big Burger*."

"I believe I see where you are headed with this," said Jim. "He'll be listening to the crew, and watching the ship. He wants to see if there are more people, who like Robbie, will have too much to drink and start talking; not to say that Robbie gave him any good info, but he's watching the ship to make sure the gas rounds stay on board."

"You got it," said Phil. "We will be watching and listening too."

"How do you plan to do that, and stay unseen at the same time?" Sam quizzed.

"Simple, your agents are still on board, right? I have some good contacts there too. Get a message to your people and have them contact Petty Officer Fitzpatrick; we will have all the eyes and ears on the beach we will need. Make sure they are aware of the security level of all this activity. Gail, when the time is right, you will have to contact Timekeeper and get his people involved. Inform them of our plan. They can get things in motion for all arrangements on the ship; things like, notifying the Captain of our intent, the pilots ready, the Master at Arms and his jail cell to put Masawi in; and the possibility of getting us out of a Greek one. Once we get into Athens and find this guy, we can set things into motion."

"Roger that," said Gail. "How much of the pharmaceutical do we have to work with?"

"We have enough Ketamine in there to keep him knocked out for hours," said Phil. "You should notice a red set and a green set of syringes and vials. We use the green one first. That is the Ketamine. The green syringes are used with it. They are marked with the maximum dosage for his estimated weight, just enough to knock him out. The red ones are DSIP or Deep Sleep Inducing Peptide, similarly marked. That one is used to maintain his sleep for a while longer.

Jim said, "I took a sneak peek in the bag, I think we'll be ok with what we have."

"I think you're right, Jimmy boy," said Sam. "I checked out the bag too, and there is enough."

"We have to be very careful with how long we keep him under. There could be a problem with dehydration, especially under the back seat. We do not have an IV bag, so hopefully we can get him to the ship in just a couple of hours."

"What if we can't?" asked Gail.

"Well we'll have to let him regain consciousness, just long enough to give him liquids, then put him back under. Let's hope that isn't necessary."

"I would ask you, how you know all of this," said Gail, "but that too can wait, until we get around to our 'long talk' someday."

Jim said, "That talk appears to be getting longer and longer each day we are here."

Sam said, "I'd like to be around to hear that discussion."

Gail responded, "You're invited."

They continued the difficult drive down to Athens, while studying the pictures of the known associates of Mohamed Masawi.

# CHAPTER 31

**WHEN THEY REACHED ATHENS,** they headed off in search of the Glyfada Hotel. The quartet acquired a suite for the week. With adjoining rooms, this would provide flexibility, and serve two purposes; first security, and second, convenience of operational necessities. They set about moving their equipment into the rooms and preparing to hunt down, or attract, the infamous *waiter*.

After getting settled in, Jim suggested they drive around a bit and get familiar with their surroundings. In the process of touring around, the team took notes on traffic patterns, foot traffic, number of police patrolling, bus and taxi availability. Anything that could be used to their advantage, in capturing and spiriting Masawi out of the country, was noted.

"Anyone hungry?" asked Jim.

"Yes," responded Phil. "I think it's time to visit the Big Burger for a bite to eat."

"Great idea," said Sam. "That'll give us a chance to scope the place out, before it gets filled with our crewmates."

"This brings up another point. What's going to be our cover-story, if we cross paths with any of them?" asked Gail.

Phil said, "According to our orders, we're tourists. I think what we'll say is, that we decided to take leave after they took us off the ship."

"I'm not sure that is the best story," Sam said, "but I guess it's better than the truth. No one would believe the truth anyway."

Phil looked over his shoulder at Sam and said, "The truth being stranger than fiction?"

"Yes, exactly," she said.

The Mercedes circled the Big Burger two times. Phil pulled it into a parking spot in front of the restaurant, not trying to avoid being seen. "Time to let everyone know we're here," said Phil. With that, they all clamored out of the automobile, attracting the attention of several restaurant patrons that were sitting outside on the patio. Each of them cautiously scanned the area, taking in every detail possible, looking especially for anyone who appeared to be paying particular attention to them.

A tall middle aged waiter approached them. "Seating for four?" he asked in English, but with a definite Greek accent.

"Thank you," responded Phil. "That will be fine." The waiter speaking English to them off the bat indicated, their lack of trying to hide who they were, *American tourists*, had worked.

"My name is Georgiou. May I start you off with a drink?" he asked.

"Jim, *Cassia de red grape*?" asked Phil. The others laughed, while the waiter obviously didn't understand the joke.

"No, I think I'll have the Greek brusco, a carafe Georgiou."

"A carafe?" said Sam.

"Yes, enough to share with the three of you; try a glass of this creation, a hearty red, and it's delicious."

"Does it go with a cheeseburger?" asked Gail.

"Absolutely," said the waiter.

"Then bring us cheeseburgers all around, along with French fries," she said.

"While we're waiting for the order," Jim said, "I'm going to browse around a little."

"I'll browse with you." Sam said.

"Ok, but not the men's room please," he cautioned. The two started off to the restroom area, Jim went right, and Sam went left. Phil observed that Georgiou had paid particular attention to them. Sam emerged from the lady's room and made sure no one was watching her. She quietly slipped to the back of the restaurant where she found the back door; it was unlocked and out of sight of the kitchen and patrons.

She slipped through the door, and stepped out into an alleyway; it was open on both ends and connected to the streets they had circled on earlier. This could be the escape point if needed she thought.

She was standing there surveying the alley when a young worker came out to dump a garbage container. He stopped; startled at first, then he continued and smiled at her.

Jim came through the door; taking notice of the situation, he moved over to Sam's side. Quickly he slipped his hand around her waist and pulled her to him. Within a moment, he placed a lingering passionate kiss on her soft and willing lips. The worker watched the couple for a brief moment, finishing his task, he returned to the restaurant.

Sam opened her eyes to make sure the worker wasn't still there. "He's gone," she tried to whisper, but the kiss continued. She moved her arms around Jim's body. Finally, the kiss parted slowly. She said, "I think it worked."

"I think you're right, but to make sure," he pulled her closer to him and their lips met again.

"Starting to worry about you guys," Gail said.

Phil, noticing tell-tell remnants of the kiss, smiled at Jim and made a subtle motion toward his lips. Jim turned and tried to erase the lipstick evidence; but not before Gail's sharp eyes had detected it. She pretended not to notice as she turned and winked at Phil. He smiled at her.

Phil said, "Georgiou was watching you two closely as you left the table. You didn't get caught snooping, did you?"

"Snooping no, but one of the kitchen helpers came out to dump trash as I was surveying the alleyway out back. Jim came out right after him and, well improvised."

"I think he was convinced by our performance, that we were harmless," said Jim.

"I see," said Phil. He looked to Gail, and they both smiled knowing what Sam meant by improvised.

"We have about twenty four hours before the ship arrives. After we eat, we can scout out a route back to the dock area. We need to establish the exact point, where the ships boats will be offloading the liberty parties. That will be our egress point with our cargo."

The waiter approached with their food.

"Your order my friends." He placed each plate on the table working his way to the ladies first. "There is an American ship coming in tomorrow, are you aware?"

This momentarily caught them off guard. Recovering quickly though, Jim announced, "Yes, it is our ship, we are on leave," pointing at Phil, who's eyes had widened after Loves statement. "Our wives are here touring with us," gesturing toward Gail and Samantha. "We are traveling port to port ahead of the ship. That is the only way the Captain would let us take leave."

"Good plan," the waiter stated. "If he needs you, you are close."

"Yes," said Phil. "He likes to keep us under his thumb."

"Yes, I see. If there is anything more you need, please ask."

"Well there is one more thing; do you know where the ships boats will be landing to bring the crew ashore?"

"Yes, it is the small port pier, at the end of Grigoriou Lampraki. It is just south of the golf course; easy to find. We call it, in English, Fleet Landing, there is a marker." With that, he returned to the kitchen.

"Do you think he's part of a European waiter's union, or some other network?" Jim asked.

The others gave him the old, *'are you kidding,'* wrinkled brow look.

"Seriously, was it a coincidence that Masawi was working as a waiter in Palma? Didn't you think this guy acted a little suspiciously?"

Sam's expression changed, "Damn, Love, you may be on to something. We'll have to keep that in mind, no matter what."

"Thank you love," Jim quipped. Sam smiled sheepishly at him.

Gail spoke, "If that is the case, then that would give him good cover everywhere in Europe and the Mid-East. This may work out for us after all. The fact that we are here, will travel faster through a network." They were in agreement, and trusted that it was the case.

"Now about that, *'our wives'*, part Jim?" Gail asked. "Where did that come from?"

"It just seemed the natural thing to say in the situation."

Gail looked at Phil, "Well where is my diamond, hubby?"

Sam joined, "Yea, hubby. Don't you have a credit card, for my diamond?"

Jim looked at Phil for help. "It wasn't my idea Love, but it is a great cover story; and by the way ladies don't wear their jewelry while on tour here, thievery you know."

Sam said, "Sounds like a load of bull to me. You're just trying to cheat a girl out of what she deserves."

Phil said. "You've created a monster Jim, and I am referring to the cover story, just to make sure everyone understands." Sam and Gail both stood up and said "Thank you for the burgers," and they waited outside for the guys to pay the bill. The guys chuckled. Then Jim said, "I think yours is serious." He said as he walked out to join the ladies.

Jim knew this would get to Phil, and he was chuckling inside, remembering what Phil had said earlier that day about having fun; it had stuck with him. *There is always danger, but time for fun too.*

Having finished the American style burgers, and Greek brusco, they were off in search of the fleet landing.

## CHAPTER 32

**FINDING THE PIER AND** landing area was fairly easy. They simply followed the waiter's directions.

Gail spotted a public phone next to the pier, and said to the others. "I think now would be a good time to contact Timekeeper and give him an update. As I look around, there doesn't appear anyone is hanging out, but maybe those two, half way down the pier fishing."

Sam, Jim and Phil surveyed the area individually and agreed. Gail reached in her pocket for the card Timekeeper had given her, and exited the vehicle. She picked up the handset and dialed the number, the others stood watch.

"Good evening," said the voice on the other end of the line. "I have been waiting for your call. Do you have an update for me?" It was Timekeeper himself.

"Yes," said Gail. "We've been busy surveying the…,"

"I know what you've been doing," he said. "Do you have an update?" She gave him the details of the plan they had concocted.

"Very well, keep in touch, by the way, how was your burger?" asked Timekeeper; and he disconnected.

Gail returned to the others and reported the conversation to them. "Timekeeper is a bit of a grump," she said. "Before he hung the phone up, he asked me how my burger was. How did he know what I had to eat?"

Phil said, "They are keeping a close eye on us. He probably knows our every move before we make it. You know he can't be directly involved, but that doesn't mean he can't keep close surveillance; and he can pull us out of a fire if need be."

The four returned to the hotel, met in Phil and Gail's room. There they formulated a plan for the next day, and reviewed the photographs of Masawi's friends and associates.

"Check this picture out," Sam said. "This could be the waiter at the Big Burger, minus a few pounds and a few years." Phil looked at the picture and passed it to the others.

Jim said, "Again Sam, I think you're on to something." With this discovery, the decision was made to remain in the general area of the hotel and the Big Burger restaurant, in hopes of increasing their chances of getting seen by Masawi.

They didn't have to wait very long. About two hours into their stroll around the city, and the local shops, Phil noticed that a young boy had been following them for several blocks. He alerted the others, and they began to maneuver around to get a look at him. He was about five and a half feet tall, and maybe one hundred and thirty pounds.

Sam said to Jim, "Isn't that the worker that was in back of the burger place yesterday?"

Jim said, "The one and the same, think he wants to see if what he witnessed yesterday was legitimate?"

Sam smiled and took his hand. Then she turned and gave him a kiss that startled Gail and Phil. But in doing so, she was able to snap a picture with the small camera she retrieved from the bag of tricks.

Gail noticed what she had done and immediately said, "Knock it off you two lovebirds, there will be plenty of time for that later."

Phil was still partially stunned when Gail took him by the hand and led him on down the street. "Sam took a picture of the guy," said Gail.

Phil said, "It looked like more than a photo opportunity to me."

"So what if it was?" said Gail. "Two birds with one stone is never a bad option."

The four continued down the street appearing to be, the ordinary American tourists they were portraying.

"Did you get what you wanted Sam?" asked Phil.

"Sure did, a full face shot."

"Yeah, I noticed the full face thing," laughed Phil.

"Where do I fit in here?" Jim asked.

Gail said, "You were just the happy medium through which all this happened."

Sam said, "You were the willing subordinate, without you, I couldn't have done it."

"Sam," said Jim. "Take some more pictures, please!"

Outwardly they were performing like true American tourists, not a care in the world, and enjoying the day. But now they had to make a drop, and get the film to Timekeeper.

The ship was scheduled to arrive in port at noon local time. Jim suggested they go back and get the car and drive to the water front. In doing that, they could find a spot nearby, and observe the crowd that was sure to gather and watch as the ship arrived.

"I'm sure Samantha wants to take more pictures," said Jim. "I wish she had a movie camera too."

"You are too much," said Samantha.

After retrieving the car Jim drove them to a spot north of the landing; they parked the Mercedes and walked the last quarter mile to the waterfront. Once in place, and satisfied with the makeshift cover, they felt suitably hidden from the general view; they sat and waited for the ship to arrive.

The locals were starting to gather anticipating the ships arrival. Some set up tables where trinkets and perfumes were placed. Others set up food carts with everything from ice cream to gyros. They hoped to attract the sailors coming from the ship, and separate them from their money.

As more people trickled in, the four began to filter through the faces, looking for anyone that they may have seen before, or recognized from the photographs. They were mostly looking for any of the known associates of Masawi as each of them had studied the pictures provided, in their *bag of tricks*. Now they were employing this knowledge in an effort to give their team the advantage.

"Have you ever thought about what you will do after the Navy?" asked Gail.

Phil looked at her and asked, "Where did that come from?"

"I don't know," she said. "It just crossed my mind, I've been thinking about the future much more lately. Not just because of what we are involved in now, but since you came into my life."

"That's a good question," Phil responded. "It isn't that far away, you know, retirement. We have to make it through this first though."

"We?" she asked.

"Well yes, that is if you don't plan on kicking me to the curb. I like having you around me, you make me a better person, and I want to do things for you, and with you."

She gazed into his eyes, and could see the sincerity deep within. She knew what she wanted for the rest of her life too, and it was him. He reached out his hand to her but was interrupted by Sam.

"No time for that now, the waiter is here. Look at the old guy in tattered clothing, that's him, over my right shoulder. Jim looked over her shoulder and spotted him crossing the road."

"Nice disguise," Gail said. "But piss poor timing."

"We, Jim and I, are going to get close to him." Sam said. "We're going to talk about how good the Big Burger is, and that we plan to go back there tonight and every night until we leave Athens. We're counting on him picking up on that, and maybe showing his face around there."

"Where do we go from there?" asked Gail.

"Don't know; we haven't made that part up yet. I've got to get back to Jim." After that she scurried off to rejoin her partner, leaving Phil and Gail, to improvise on their own.

The Mt Mitchell had moved gently to within a half mile of the pier; she would anchor there. This provides the ship with plenty of room for the swing arc. The ship would need this room to allow her to swing around on the anchor as the tide changed direction. This action is not unlike a weather vane turning in the wind. Once again the loud rattling and clanking of the anchor being dropped was heard, but this time for the ones on shore, the sound reverberated in the distance, and echoed lightly off building walls.

Sam and Jim had moved within earshot of Masawi. Phil and Gail watched closely, unobserved by their target.

Sam said, "Jim you must take me back to that American burger place. I wouldn't mind eating there every night until we leave Athens. And besides it is just a short walk from the Glyfada Hotel where we're staying."

"If you insist, and as long as you are happy, that's what matters to me." They moved away, confident that the information had not fallen on deaf ears.

They strolled north away from the pier, where they rejoined the other half of the team. "How did it go?" asked Phil.

Sam said, "A bit corny, but I think we got the point across."

Jim said, "The bureau, nor the service, offer acting classes. Let's get far enough away so we can stop and keep an eye on this bastard."

For the next twenty minutes, Masawi pretended to be interested in the American ship in the harbor, and then he slowly moved away from the main crowd, and shuffled up Grigoriou Lampraki; the street leading away from the waterfront, and toward the Big Burger and The Glyfada Hotel.

## CHAPTER 33

**GLYFADA HOTEL; READ THE** marquee above the spot where Jim parked the Mercedes. Gail took Phil's hand as she exited the automobile. "We have a conversation to finish after we get this creep." "Yes we do," Phil said. "For now we've got to remain focused."

After exiting the car, they turned to say something to Jim, but he and Sam were entwined in each other's arms and sharing another passionate kiss. They parted, turned toward the car and looking across the top at the other two. Phil and Gail were watching them. It was as if the two agents were on stage, performing in front of a live audience.

"What?" Jim said, "We can't let you two have all the fun." Sam smiled, pointed at Gail and winked.

"I think she's indicating that this is entirely your fault," Phil said.

"You don't speak girl talk or sign language, do you?" Gail asked. "She just said I was right all along, and thank you."

"You got all that from a simple finger point?"

"She winked too, or didn't you notice?"

"I've got a lot more to learn," he said.

141

They trailed along behind Sam and Jim, who at this time were half way to their room.

"I think they are eager to get to the restaurant," Gail stated.

"I'll take your word for that this time," answered Phil.

Sam turned and called to them, "Stop dragging your feet, we need to get changed and head for the Big Burger, time is of the essence."

Gail was grinning, as Phil looked at her and shook his head side to side.

"Knock on the inside door when you're ready," Gail said. Sam gave her the thumbs up.

"I understood that one," Phil joked.

"You are a quick study my love," she said.

As the door closed behind them, they began to prepare for the evening.

The expected knock on the door came, and Sam said "Are you guys' descent?"

Gail opened the door, "Come on in, Phil's putting his shoes on, then we can go."

Phil finished tying his shoes and stood up. "I don't think we need to try and take this guy tonight. We need to observe and do a mock walk through, you know, find out what he does there, if anything, and where he goes when he leaves; but more importantly, if he has back-up. I know we were told he works alone, but I want to make sure of that."

"Yeah, that's a great point, I certainly don't want to run into any friends he may have picked up along the way," said Jim.

"We can take it slow and easy tonight, and just observe everyone. I'm hoping Timekeeper got our message to the ship," stated Sam.

Gail had to get her two cents worth in, "Me too, and I'm with you guys." Off to the Big Burger they went to eat drink and observe.

While walking to the restaurant, Sam asked Jim, "What part do you think the man that was following us plays in all of this?"

"He's probably just a worker at the Big Burger that Georgiou sent out to tail us. I don't think he's had any training in finer art of shadowing people. Especially as easily as Phil spotted him; not taking away from your prowess Phil; and considering how easily you, Sam, were able to take his picture."

"You didn't seem to mind," Sam stated.

Jim chuckled and said, "Want to practice that move some more?"

"Maybe later she said, with a smile on her face. "We've got some snooping to do first. By the way, I prepared a message with instructions for my agents. I am instructing them to be available each night here at the restaurant, but to remain uninvolved, until such time as we may need them. I just have to figure a way to get the message to one of them." They continued to the Big Burger. This time requested seats outside on the patio.

About an hour or so had passed since the ship anchored, and a few of the ship's crewmembers were making their way into the streets of Glyfada. A few of the neighboring establishments in the vicinity had attracted some of the American sailors, but a number of the younger ones were focusing on the Big Burger, and its American Style food.

A different waiter, a younger man, more Mid-Eastern in appearance, assisted the team tonight. "Is Georgiou here tonight?" Phil asked.

"No, not tonight," he answered hesitantly. "Why do you ask?"

"I just wanted to thank him for the directions he gave us to the landing yesterday, it was very helpful."

"I see. May I take your order?" This new waiter didn't seem to have much of a friendly personality, as noted by all four in the group. They ordered a variety of dishes, and the Greek brusco

143

that Jim had introduced to them the night before. Gail, of course ordered the obligatory cheeseburger and fries.

As they were enjoying their meal, a white four-door Mercedes sedan pulled off the street and into the alleyway running behind the restaurant. Sam noticed it and said, "Please excuse me, I must visit the ladies room." Phil had noticed it too.

"Watch your step," Phil said. "You Bet' cha!" she said. As she stepped away from the table, Phil informed the other two on what they had noticed.

"Gail," Jim called, "If she's not back in a couple of minutes, check on her." She was ready to do just that, when Sam came strolling back to the table.

"The passenger in the white car is our target. I turned out the light in the ladies room, watched and listened at the window. Our waiter was talking to him. Without a translator I couldn't tell what they were saying, but I did here the term 'Americans' used a couple of times."

"Looks as if our plan is working up to this point, where do we go from here?" asked Gail. "Whatever we do, proceed cautiously is what I'm thinking."

Sam said, "Well would you look at that, no don't, do not look," she said quickly. "It's Kathryn, my senior agent in training, and Fitzpatrick, your guy Phil, out on a date."

"Appears our backup eyes and ears have arrived," Phil said. " Timekeeper must have gotten through."

"Now all I have to do is get this message to one of them," said Sam. She and Fitzpatrick locked eyes, in an instant Sam signaled with her eyes to the empty table beside them. Fitz picked up the hint and gently nudged Kathryn in that direction.

Kathryn took the lead from there. They exchanged smiles and friendly greetings with everyone in the patio area, careful not to focus on the four seated at the table beside them. The waiter came to the table and took their order. He glanced at Sam a couple of times. Everyone was on guard, watching for anyone paying undue attention to them. The waiter walked back toward the kitchen; Sam scribbled a note and slipped it into Kathryn's bag; she had hung it open and conveniently on the side of her chair that faced toward Sam. Sam whispered, "Good job, training pays off again. Don't read it until you leave this place."

Jim was playing along too. He was holding Sam's hand and pretending she was talking to him. No one had seemed to notice the exchange.

The four finished their food and wine. As they rose to leave, and Jim was leaving money for the bill, Phil looked over to Fitzpatrick and said, "The two of you enjoy your evening, it's a romantic atmosphere."

"Thank you Ss…, Sir, that's kind of you." Fitz had almost called his boss by his military title, but caught himself in time. Phil broke a faint smile, and walked away.

Walking back to the hotel, they noticed a car had been slowly following them, keeping an adequate distance behind, so as not to give them opportunity to see anyone inside the vehicle. The street was slightly uphill and strung with banners and flags practically all the way back to the hotel.

They were about two blocks from the hotel, when a second car came sliding around the corner and accelerated directly at them. Jim instinctively pushed everyone into one of the recessed doorways, and faced the oncoming car alone. He started to reach for his Makarov when his instincts told him to look up instead; dangling in front of him was a strand of excess cable used to hold the banners across the street. He grabbed the cable and hoisted himself up, as a pole-vaulter would. Love pulled himself up the cable, kicking his feet high into the air, just as the speeding car passed.

Sam and Phil had both retrieved their weapons and were empting the 9mm magazines into the back of the car. The windows were shattering, one tire flattened by one of Sam's shots, but the white Mercedes sedan kept going. As it disappeared around the corner, they shifted their focus to the first car that had been following them, but it was gone also.

Instinctively they turned to check on Jim; Gail was helping him off of the pavement.

"Jim, are you alright?" Sam asked, as she hurried back to him.

"I'm good, just a little dirty from the fall, good thing I have a hard head."

They looked down; the cable that Jim had used to hoist himself up and over the car with was lying on the street. It had parted the split second after the car passed under him.

Jim quipped, "I guess they know we're in town. What is it with white Mercedes?"

"I don't know, but we'd better get out of here and off the streets before the police show up. With this ruckus, someone must have called them by now. Come on sweetie, I've got to get you cleaned up." Sam said.

They all but sprinted the last two blocks back to the hotel, slowing only after they reached the property.

"Let me get him cleaned up a bit, then you guys come over for a nightcap. We need to finalize a plan quickly," said Sam. She took Jim by the arm and started him toward the room.

"I'm ok 'sug'," he said as Sam was rubbing his back.

"That could have been catastrophic had it not been for Jims quick action," said Phil. "He just saved our lives, and risked his own in the process."

"I agree, he's what one would call a hero, and Sam calls sweetie." Gail hugged Phil tightly. They stood there for a moment, embraced in each other's arms, thankful for the outcome.

# CHAPTER 34

**AFTER MAKING THEIR WAY** back to their rooms, they took a few minutes to gather their senses and piece together what had just happened. A knock came at the adjoining suite door. Samantha opened it. Gail asked, "How's our hero?"

Sam, not totally over the event and still partially shaken answered, "He's a little scratched up and bruised, but I think he will make a full recovery. That fall from about seven feet or so onto the brick street was harsh to say the least."

"I'm fine; in fact, I think we should go back out and find that bullet-ridden automobile, and check it for blood. I'm convinced one of you put a round into him."

Sam jumped in, "You need to take a hot bath and soak for a while, if you don't, you're going to be awfully sore in the morning."

Phil said to Jim, "She's right, we can take this up again tomorrow bright and early."

Jim insisted, "The trail will grow cold, we need to find that car, and find out who was driving it."

"Ok," said Phil. "Gail and I will take the Mercedes for a spin around town in the probable areas around the Big Burger and see what we can find. You follow you nurse's orders." With that said, Jim agreed reluctantly to Phil's suggestion.

"Just don't do anything rash," said Sam.

"Not to worry," said Gail. "I'll keep him under control." They closed the door and headed down to the car.

Driving in the direction of the incident, they noticed police at the scene investigating what had occurred. Phil turned the car onto a side street and proceeded to go around the police. He then made another turn to put them back on track to follow the last known direction of the car that had tried to run them down; they didn't have to go far.

Only two blocks from where they had lost sight of the white sedan, there it was. Police were all around the automobile, some with pistols still in hand. Phil drove a close as possible until a policeman motioned him to stop. He approached them.

"What is your business here?" the policeman asked.

Phil answered, "We're driving down to the pier to look at the American ship with all the lights on, it is supposed to be a romantic sight."

"Is there something we can help with here officer?" Gail asked.

"No," responded the officer. "Continue on your way, but drive slowly around the crash, I have officers all over and it is dark." With that they gave a nod to the officer and proceeded forward.

"See if you can tell who was driving the car, maybe we have seen him before." Gail strained to see the face turned toward the window and laying on the steering wheel.

She gasped, "My God, it's the guy that was following us, the restaurant worker. He's dead for sure; no one is in a hurry to get him out of the car, and there is blood everywhere. We need to get back to the hotel and update Jim and Sam."

Phil told Gail she needed to make an update to Timekeeper

and fill him in on everything since their last communication. The Mercedes continued on the path toward the pier.

"You can use the same phone as last time. It seems to be a secure area and is easy to watch for interlopers."

Gail slipped from the front seat and walked the short distance to the phone. Phil waited by the driver's side of the car, keeping the Mercedes between him and the street. He noticed a police car cruising nearby. It made a detour into the lot at the end of the pier. It was the officer that had spoken to them at the scene of the accident. Gail completed the update with Timekeeper and had just returned to Phil's side. She slipped her arm around him and placed a lingering kiss on his lips. This seemed to pacify the police officer, they indeed had made their way to see the romantic seaside lights of Glyfada, and the lights of the American ship anchored in the harbor. "Perfect timing," whispered Phil. Gail smiled up at him and kissed his lips again, this time with more passion and intent.

"The first one was for him, that one was for me," she said. "Now let's get back to the hotel for the update. Timekeeper has some news for us."

"What is it?" Phil asked.

"It can wait," she teased.

Gail knocked at the connecting door to Sam's room. Sam opened the door slowly. She slipped through it, and closed the door behind her.

"He's asleep; I put him in the tub and washed and dressed his wounds. He'll be ok in the morning."

"How are you?" Gail asked.

"I'm good, just glad that cable was there, for a brief time anyway."

"Absolutely! We found the car that was used to run us down, the driver was the man in the picture you took; the worker from the restaurant."

'The one following us on the street today?" Sam asked.

"Yes the very one, and one of you made the shot that took him out. He made it only about two blocks around the corner. The police are everywhere. We were stopped and questioned, Phil made up this story about going down to the pier to view the romantic lights."

"Somehow I figured he would check out our story, so we drove on to the pier and Gail contacted Timekeeper. She gave him an update to include tonight's events. As soon as she was off the phone the police officer passed through the parking lot. I think Gail convinced him the romantic lights were what we had come to see."

Sam said, "I'll bet she did."

Phil continued, "She has something for us too."

Gail began, "He said this event tonight will all turn out to be considered a gang related incident between local Greek rivals. We are not to be concerned about the authorities coming after us. He also said we could step up our timetable for taking out Masawi. The ship is ready to assist on anything we need. Although the liberty boats will secure at midnight, they will be in standby mode if we need them. The helos are also on stand-by. Timekeeper wants him off the street. He also wants the film; here is where we are to drop it."

She showed the address to them. "The US Embassy?" Phil asked.

"We are to actually drop it in the drive way, making sure it goes behind the gate, as we walk by pretending to take pictures. There will be a Marine Guard there to pick it up at precisely 0930 tomorrow morning.

"We had better get some sleep, it's been a busy day, and we don't know what tomorrow has in store for us."

---

The next morning at coffee, Jim was briefed by Phil on the events of the preceding evening. He was beginning to heal from the minor scratches and physically he was feeling much better.

The team had made their way to the US Embassy. They were looking like the typical tourist, with coffee and cameras in hand; they made their way alongside the main gate. Phil was timing their stroll, as to put them at the gate at exactly 0930.

They moved toward the gate, Gail was fumbling with her camera as if she was trying to change the film. There was a Marine Guard in a starched and pressed uniform, and a man dressed in civilian work cloths. He was carrying a dust pan on a long handle and a broom.

Gail fumbled the roll of film; it fell through the gate and on to the Embassy property. The sweeper stepped in quick as a flash, and brushed it into the covered dust pan before the marine could respond. Gail looked on in a panic; she knew that she had botched the hand off. The sweeper reached into the dust pan and pulled out a roll of film; he handed it to the marine.

The marine stepped to the gate and said, "Your film ma'am." She reached out for the film. At this point she thought things had gone totally wrong.

She said, "No, you don't understand." The sweeper stopped and turned to look at her, and the marine just looked at her with slight confusion.

Phil took her by the arm. "Come on clumsy, take your film roll," he said to Gail.

"Thank you sir," he said to the marine. The sweeper turned and slowly walked away sweeping as he went.

"I was under the impression we were to leave the film?" said Gail.

"We did," answered Jim. "The sweeper switched the film, gave you a new roll, and took the exposed one. The Marine Guard was an innocent bystander in all this.

Recognize the sweeper?" "Timekeeper," Sam stated.

# CHAPTER 35

**BACK IN THE MERCEDES** and heading for the hotel, Samantha asked Phil, "How are we to get the name of the person in the picture? And where do we proceed from here?"

Phil glanced into the rear view mirror at her and smiled, "If I'm guessing right there is a message for us contained on the film that Timekeeper returned to us."

He looked at Gail and said, "Pull the film out of the roll and see if there is anything written on it." She did as he instructed. As she pulled the film out carefully, a message began to appear. "It's a hand written note on the back of the film," she blurted out. Gail read the message as she pulled the film from the container.

"Continue to close in on Masawi-take no chances but apprehend earliest-info will come to your room-max flexibility planned."

"What does all this mean?" Gail asked.

"I think they're getting antsy for us to get this guy before he moves on," said Jim.

"I think you hit the nail on the head. With one of their guys dead now, they may be nervous about exposure," Sam said.

Gail asked, "What about the rest of the message, what does that mean?"

Phil said. "Any updates on the terrorist will be passed to us at the hotel, probably in a note under the door. The last part means they are watching us closely and will respond to any assistance we need, without compromising themselves, in order to pull this operation off. Timekeeper and his crew probably have run every possible scenario, and have planned for any contingency. I think we need to search for a quiet place to have a late breakfast, later we can go to the Big Burger and hang out for the rest of the day. I'm sure the word has reached Masawi that it was the four Americans that killed his man; in fact, he may have been in the other car that was following us. He may have been witness to the entire event, if so he will come for us himself."

Jim asked, "Is the bag of tricks ready."

"In the trunk," said Phil. "After breakfast we can check back at the hotel for any update on our man in the picture, and formulate a loose plan for tonight."

"Loose plan?" Samantha asked.

"Absolutely," answered Phil, "We don't have any sort of timetables on Masawi, we will have to have to be reactive with our plan, and take him at the time we think will be our best opportunity to pull this off. Who's good at giving injections?"

"I can do that," Gail said. Everyone looked at her with surprise, "What?" she said. "My uncle was diabetic. He let me give him injections now and then, I got very good at it."

"You never cease to amaze me," Phil said.

"That's a good thing," Gail said.

Following their late breakfast, the four went back to the hotel to check for any messages. As the group approached the rooms, Sam noticed the cleaning crew in her room.

She said to Gail. "It looks like we'll have to join you guys for coffee until our room is cleaned."

"Good," said Gail. "We can sit on the patio for a while and chat without the boys listening in on us."

"Jim my friend, I guess we're on our own for a few minutes, take a walk by the pool?"

"Sure, that sounds inviting. We'll be back in a few minutes." He shouted to the women. They nodded their heads and waived them off. Phil stepped into the hall and noticed the service cart had been pushed aside next to the wall.

"It looks as if your room is finished," said Phil.

"Yeah, but the maids cart is still here."

About the time he finished his sentence, a different maid came around the corner, fussing and throwing her hands up in the air. She went straight to the abandoned cart, took it by the handle and started pushing it off in the direction where she had just came.

"That is just a little bizarre," Phil said.

Jim slipped his Makarov pistol from under his shirt and pointed to the door of his room. Phil took the key Jim handed to him, and slowly opened the door. Both men stood inside the door looking at a room that had not been made up. Looking around slowly Jim said, "On the dresser."

There was a large sealed envelope with nothing on the outside. He moved quickly to open it. "It's the picture of our terrorist; his name was Imad Masawi, nephew of Mohamed Masawi, our target."

"We've got to inform Sam and Gail right away. There is more in here, let's go to your room."

Phil looked around the room at the scene, especially the bed. "Looks like someone did a lot of tossing and turning last night."

Jim quipped, "Yep, my back was bothering me." With that said, Jim knocked on the adjoining suite door. Gail opened it.

"I thought you two were going for a walk by the pool."

"Changed our minds," Jim said as he handed the envelope to her. She opened the top and slid the picture out.

"That was damn quick service for film development. Oh my goodness, this guy is a relative of our terrorist."

"Was," Phil corrected. "From now on it will be imperative to watch each other's back; this guy will be out to get us all."

"Maybe this will work in our favor though," said Sam. "It may make him a bit careless."

"Careless or not Sam," said Jim. "He is still a poisonous snake."

"Agreed," responded Sam. "But we will have to be swift and accurate. Everyone check your weapons, Gail put the syringes in your carry bag now; we won't have much time later to look for anything.

"Well team, it appears the time we've been working toward is here. Take no unnecessary risks, but once we move, we must stay in motion. Is everybody ready for a fun time at the Big Burger tonight?" Phil asked.

"Only you would put it that way," Gail said. "But yes, I'm ready."

"Us too," came the assurance from Sam and Jim.

Phil parked the Mercedes just off the end of the alleyway that ran behind the restaurant. This kept it out of sight but quickly accessible for a speedy get away. They walked around the block so as to approach the front of the restaurant from a different direction from where they parked. Phil noticed several of the crewmembers present, including Kathryn and Fitzpatrick. The others quickly noticed their presents. Quick non lingering pleasantries were exchanged. Sam positioned herself at the table so as to be adjacent to Kathryn.

Kathryn held her menu in front of her face, "Your target has been in and out of here twice in the last hour. Is something going on tonight?"

Sam slapped Jim on the shoulder and said jokingly as she was answering a question from him, "I wouldn't' be surprised." This caught Jim momentarily off guard, but he recovered quickly and started laughing and agreeing with Sam. They seemed to be having a good time like everyone else at the restaurant.

Phil saw that their waiter from the last visit, Georgiou, was on the way over to their table. "Hello my friends, welcome back, I was afraid you would not return after trouble the other night."

Jim looked at him unshaken by the comment and asked, "What trouble are you talking about? Everything seemed fine when we were here."

Georgiou said, "My friends, there was a gang shooting just down the block, it has kept many patrons from here. I am glad to see you back, and that all is well with you."

"Thank you Georgiou," said Phil. "That is very thoughtful of you."

"Enough talk of such unpleasantness; what may I bring you to eat and drink." Gail spoke up, "Cheeseburgers and Brusco is fine with me."

Jim said, "Just don't blame it on me, and since I am the one who introduced Brusco to you; the same for me Georgiou." They all chuckled and it was Cheeseburgers and Brusco all around.

"Did you notice the friendlier Georgiou tonight?" asked Gail.

"I certainly did," said Sam. What's up with that?"

Jim said, "I don't know, but stay alert, I'm not sure if he is friend or foe."

About fifteen minutes into the meal, Phil noticed a white Mercedes sedan pull around the block. He informed the others quietly that their target may be arriving. Within a few moments Masawi slipped quietly into the kitchen. Gail watched as he came in through the hallway from the back door.

"Wonder where he parked," asked Sam. Fitzpatrick, picked up on the question, he slid back from the table and eased his way to the restroom. A few moments later he came back and repositioned himself at the table.

"You know Kate; I didn't know how crowded the right side of this building could be." She simply looked at him and nodded in agreement. Now they knew where his car was parked.

Jim stood up and stretched. "Think I'll move around a little, my back is bothering me." He moved slowly out to the sidewalk and to the side of the building where Masawi's car was parked. He looked around as he slipped one of the throwing knives from his ankle holster that he had removed from the bag of tricks earlier. He pushed it slowly into the left side front tire. Within a couple of seconds the tire was completely flat. Jim continued his stroll to the rear of the restaurant, and silently entered the back door. He moved unseen to the restroom, where he flushed the toilet and ran the water as if all was normal.

"Left front next to the building is flat." He smiled as he rejoined his friends. "When he goes to change it, he will be trapped between the car and the wall; we can take care of him there. Sam, when all of this starts, you bring the Mercedes around." She nodded in understanding. "Gail, please be accurate with the needle, I don't want to miss anything by taking an unexpected nap."

"Not to worry Jim. By the way, is there an antidote, in case I …," She winked at him, "Just kidding. I'll pay the bill so the waiter doesn't call the cops on us when we all disappear."

"Good thought," said Sam.

"We probably will need transportation at about zero three thirty in the morning, is there any way we can arrange that?" Phil asked.

They all looked at each other for a moment, then Fitzpatrick stood up and said to Kate, we had better go sweetie, looks like an early morning for us. He and Kathryn had been listing intently to everything that was being said by the four next to them. With that, the connection was made for the boat ride to the ship. Now all that was to be done was to secure a passenger.

# CHAPTER 36

**THE BILL WAS PAID** and another round of Brusco was ordered primarily to justify the use of the table. Sam noticed that Georgiou was paying more attention to them.

Jim said, "He's on the move. Give him a couple of minutes to get the trunk open."

Gail said, "I'm going to the restroom to see what I can out the window."

"Be careful, don't want to spook him," said Phil. "We'll give you a couple of minutes."

She entered the bathroom and moved to a position where she could see out, without being seen." She returned to the table, "Now is the time, his head is down, and I believe he is cussing the lug nuts."

"Jim, take the back of the car, I'll get the front, Sam…," he looked around and she had gone for the car already. Phil and Gail were headed for the back door; Jim went out the front of the building. Jim moved slowly to the back of the car. Masawi noticed him from the corner of his eye. "Need help?" Jim asked.

"No, I am good." He looked up at Jim. He recognized his face, he turned to run, and that's when Phil's doubled up fist caught him square in the forehead. Dazed by this, Masawi was struggling to regain his footing when Gail administered the coup d'état. The injection of Ketamine had been delivered. Phil sensed movement, it was the waiter Georgiou. He stepped around the corner and looked down at Masawi. Masawi looked up at Georgiou and told him to call the police. He turned and started back inside.

"Where do you think you're going?" Phil asked.

"Back in to call the police, but first I have a few tables to clean; it could take me a while." He grinned and then disappeared back through the back door, but this time he closed it.

Sam arrived with the car. Gail opened the back door of the Mercedes, while Jim and Phil wrestled Masawi into the back seat. Jim ran back to the rear of the car and searched the trunk. There was a green military type bag on the left side, he quickly snatched it with his right hand and dashed off to the waiting vehicle.

Once they were all in, Sam accelerated the Benz and headed for the hotel. She parked the vehicle in a darkened spot trying to avoid attention. The guys held Masawi between them as if he was a friend that had too much to drink. Sam retrieved a blanket from the trunk and wrapped it around him in part to hide his clothing, and also to lend to the appearance of caring for a friend. Gail dashed ahead and opened the door to her room. Masawi was placed on the sofa and handcuffed to the cast iron radiator.

"What time do I have to administer the next dose?" Gail asked.

"If he starts to wake up, we'll give him another green syringe. The Ketamine probably will not last long enough for us to get him to the pier tonight, so eventually we will have to hit him with the Phenobarbital. It is dosed to his weight and physical makeup so as not to harm him, just make him sleep. That stuff can put a person into a coma if used incorrectly."

"That is not our goal?" Gail asked tongue-in-cheek.

Sam said, "I thought I saw Georgiou going back into the back door, what was that all about?"

Gail answered, "He came out to see what the ruckus was about. Our guest asked him to call the police. When he turned to walk back inside, Phil asked him where he thought he was going, he said to call the police; but he had tables to clean off first. I guess that answered the question of friend or foe."

Phil was searching the bag he had retrieved from Masawi's car trunk.

"What did you find?" asked Jim. Phil pulled a Luger thirty caliber pistol from the bag. "Check this out, NAZI markings and everything."

"The gun that killed Robinson," Gail said.

The next few hours passed quietly as the team took turns monitoring their capture. Each had taken showers and freshened up some. The time now came to move Mohamed to the dock area for further transport to the Mt Mitchell. They must now move him in darkness of night. This maneuver can sometimes draw attention because of the lack of traffic on the streets at that hour. All had done their homework prior to this time though, as that was what the first day of observation was all about. Still there could be danger.

Masawi had started to come around, so Gail fed him about eight ounces of water. He refused more, so she injected him with the Phenobarbital. His breathing was regular and all vital signs were good, so they readied him for transport.

Slipping him out the back and into the Mercedes was made easier because they had time to rest and recover from the excitement earlier. Sam was driving as they headed for the dock. She pulled onto the pier area; Phil noticed a police car moving away from the dock. "Give him a minute," he said. "See if he keeps going." The police car continued to move away from the landing.

"There is the boat," Jim said. "And it appears they are ready for us. Look at that, two Stokes stretchers with flotation devices and military police. Let me get out and walk forward. I want to see what we've got here, before we commit ourselves."

Jim stepped out of the car, walked forward about ten feet; he stopped, turned, and motioned the others forward. Sam slid the transmission into drive and moved forward cautiously.

Phil said, "Well look at that."

There was Kathryn standing there with her badge and gun on, along with two shore patrol officers, who Phil immediately recognized as members of his division on the ship. The ships corpsman was standing by, and Fitzpatrick was at the helm of the boat while also directing the operation. "Get him into the bottom stretcher, put the oxygen mask on him and cover him with a blanket; we've got company, the local police.

Sure enough it was the lonely police car they had seen earlier. He had made a trip around the block and circled back.

Fitzpatrick said, "Cover him with another blanket, and keep the oxygen mask going Doc."

They had formed a clamshell with the two stretchers and secured them together with leather straps. The police man approached the scene.

"What is the emergency here?" Gail was standing beside Phil, she sprang into action.

"We have an overdose of drugs! One of our sailors was given a heavy dose of barbiturates from here." She pointed out into the town. "We are trying to save his life." She produced the syringe that had held the Phenobarbital, and quickly gave it to the corpsman. "This should help you in determining how much and what he was given by these reckless people."

She looked at the police officer and said, "We found him with it hanging out of his arm." The officer said, "If you have it under control, is see no need for a report; it would only cause him more trouble tomorrow.

"Not to mention, the reputation of this lovely city," Sam added as she turned toward Kate who was tugging at her arm.

"Yes, well, continue your good work," the officer said and returned to his car. As he drove away, Phil looked at Jim Love and said.

"Hell of a couple of agents we have here." Jim pointed out, "Not a bad group Fitz put together either; are they authentic?"

"Mostly," Phil stood there grinning from ear to ear.

Fitzpatrick shouted out to them, "We'll turn him over to the brig crew as soon as we get back, they're waiting on us."

Sam reminded Kate, "Give this guy no slack; he is a stone cold killer. Let everyone know just how dangerous this guy is."

"Not to worry, Doc will put an IV in his arm so we can keep him under until we can get him transferred in a couple of hours."

"Great work to all of you," Sam shouted. "See you tomorrow night?" She said to Kathryn.

"As soon as this guy clears our deck, we'll be over."

The boat was loaded and headed back to the ship when Sam looked at Phil and said, "Did she say we?"

"I do believe she did." They both turned to Gail and smiled, "Did you have anything to do with this?"

She smiled sheepishly and said, "Maybe."

Phil turned back to Sam and said, "Told you she was 'The Matchmaker.'"

"Let's get back to the hotel; we have a long day tomorrow too," said Sam.

"What are you talking about? It is tomorrow," quipped Jim.

"Yes, but we have a meeting with Timekeeper at thirteen hundred at the Embassy. The other three stood looking in puzzlement at Samantha.

"This message was handed to me by Kathryn while you guys were busy with the local police. The quarterdeck watch gave it to her just before they left the ship." Sam opened the message and handed it over for the others to read. *Great work tonight-see you tomorrow thirteen hundred Embassy.*

Looking back toward the ship they noticed a small two-man helicopter lifting off from the Mt Mitchell's helo deck.

"That's strange," Jim said, "Flight ops at this hour? And the boat with Masawi on board is just now going along side."

"Do you think Timekeeper is in the helo?" Gail asked Phil. "I wouldn't doubt it for a moment."

# CHAPTER 37

**"WHERE DO YOU SEE** us going from here?" Was the first thing Jim heard the next morning; as Samantha lay in bed by his side, she watched as he tried to clear his eyes, and wake from a short night's sleep.

"Good morning to you too, my love," he said. "Well first of all I think food of some sort is in order, then the meeting with Timekeeper after that."

"You're not very quick when you first wake up are you?" she asked. "I mean us, we, the two of us. Where do we go from here? I am talking after all this secret spy episode of our lives. Is this just a short time, good time for you?"

Jim took a moment to clear the sleepiness left in his brain. "You've been awake for a while thinking about this, haven't you?"

"You must be awake now if you figured that out," she answered.

"First of all," he said. "I haven't given much thought about being without you at all; I kind 'a like having you around all the time. I personally think we make a good team, working and playing. I started, on several occasions, to tell you how I feel about you, but I didn't want to scare you off. I started to fall in love with you when our eyes first met, and a little prodding from Gail didn't hurt either. She encouraged me, but didn't push me; she really is a matchmaker you know."

"Do you think we are a match?" she asked. He studied her expression for a moment then said, "If being happy and overjoyed every day I see you, means we're closely matched, then, I think yes. But that is just my side of the equation, what are your thoughts on the subject?"

"Well, I feel like I'm looking into deep water, like I'm trying to decide whether to jump in or not, I care for you very profoundly."

He placed his hand behind her neck and drew her closer to him, "If you can swim, the depth of the water is no barrier," he placed a light kiss on her forehead. "I'm prepared to wake up with you for the rest of my life."

She looked up into his smiling face and snuggled securely into his arms. "That is a brave statement," she said.

He smiled and said, "Didn't I tell you, I was an Olympic swimmer in college?" She moved her hand across his bare chest. Holding tightly to one another, they drifted gently back to sleep.

A knock at the door adjoining the two rooms woke them from a deep sleep. "Just a minute," Sam shouted, startling Jim from his slumber. "Coming," Sam called out as she quickly wrapped her slender nude body in a terrycloth bath robe. She opened the door to see Phil standing there. His eyes widened as he was caught momentarily off guard by Samantha standing there in a bath robe.

"Sorry to interrupt, but we were wondering if you two wanted to go for breakfast with us. If you are busy..."

"No, no, we just slept in late, long night as you know. Give us a couple of minutes; better yet, we'll meet you in the dining room."

"Sounds good," Phil said. "See you there." She closed the door.

Phil turned to Gail, "I think those two are becoming an item."

"What makes you say that?"

"As long as we have been together on this assignment that is the first time I've seen her in a bath robe and she seemed comfortable with me knowing they were intimate with each other."

"Have you had your eyes closed all this time?" Gail asked. "I've known all along she was falling in love with him. I could see the expression on her face and his as well."

"I thought something was happening between them," Phil said. "I guess that moment at the door just drove it home."

"You have to stop and smell the roses some time Philip my love," as she drew him to her and placed an adoring kiss on his lips. "You may be fixating on the case excessively." This stirred the emotion in him, he smiled and said, "You make a good point, I can feel what you saying."

"Breakfast, my love, breakfast; that is what we have on the agenda first, then the meeting with Timekeeper, dessert will have to wait."

"Yeah, your right, they are going to meet us in the dining room, let's go before I get into trouble."

"So now I'm trouble am I?" Phil opened the door and waited for Gail to join him. She walked past him and slid her palm across the cheek of his face, "Follow trouble lover, and see where she leads you."

"Breakfast I hope," he chuckled. She blocked his way and pulled his shirt collar drawing his face to hers, "Watch it big boy, your dessert can be put on ice." She placed a quick kiss on his lips, released his collar and turned and headed for the dining room.

Phil shook his head, smiled and thought how much he loved her and her subtle quick humor. He followed along behind his love, thinking how lucky he was to have met her.

"So if dessert is ice cream, being put on ice is not a bad thing right?" he asked.

"Don't push it big boy, or that hot apple pie will go in the freezer." He chuckled again and decided to remain silent for the remainder of the walk to the dining room.

After reaching the breakfast area of the dining room, they ordered eggs, bacon, and fruit, for four, along with coffees all around. They chose a table overlooking the residential area and mountain range behind.

"This place has so many beautiful views," Gail said.

"Yes it does, and I love the travel down the Peloponnesian coast road. That view overlooking the Gulf of Corinth is stunning." Just as he said that, Jim and Sam joined them.

"Good morning Sleepy head," Gail said to Jim.

"What makes you so chipper this morning?" he asked.

"She's looking forward to pie and ice cream this evening," Phil said.

Gail looked at him and quipped, "Yeah, cold pie and hot ice cream for you if you keep it up." They snickered between the two of them, while Jim and Sam looked on in puzzlement. "I'll explain later," Gail said to Sam. "Me too," Phil said to Jim.

"By the way we took the liberty of ordering for you," Phil said. "It is the only thing on the menu this morning.

I guess there was a miscommunication with the kitchen staff."

"Good," Sam said. "Jimmy here has problems focusing in the morning." It was now their turn to giggle while the other two looked on in puzzlement. "I'll explain later," they both said simultaneously.

The four of them were now snickering, laughing and seemed not to have a care in the world. This was good for now, but in the back of their minds were thinking about the meeting with Timekeeper scheduled for later in the day, and what was the purpose of the meeting?

Following breakfast the team decided to spend some time actually seeing some sights of Athens. Samantha suggested the Acropolis; because of the closer location to the embassy. There they could see the Parthenon, and from up on Acropolis hill, they would have a great view of Athens.

Phil drove the team up to the foot of the Acropolis hill. They parked the Mercedes and started the trek to the top of the rocky hill. As they reached the top, there was the Parthenon in all its splendor and greatness. Phil and Gail were standing there, her arm around his waist and his arm around her shoulder. Jim and Samantha stood hand in hand admiring the greatness of the spectacular sight in front of them.

Jim turned to Sam and asked, "Would you marry me some day?"

Gail's perfect hearing didn't let her down. She turned slowly toward Phil and asked quietly, "Did you hear what I just heard?"

"I was just about to ask you the same thing."

"You mean if I heard what he said, or you were going to ask the same question he asked Sam?"

"If you heard what he said," Phil returned.

"Oh," Gail responded. They turned slowly as not to interrupt the moment.

Samantha was looking and searching deeply into Jim's eyes tying to read his thoughts. The only thing she could see was openness and honesty as she opened her mouth and said, "Someday, not Sunday, right."

"Yes, some-day." Jim said.

"Then yes, I will marry you someday."

"I've had this for a week or so, it's for you." With that he revealed a two carat diamond engagement ring. The ring setting was one carat stone in the center, surrounded by smaller stones totaling one carat. The ring was twenty four carat gold. He took her left hand and slipped the ring on her finger. He breathed a sigh, "I thought I guessed right."

"Sam reached around his neck, and planted a passionate loving kiss on his lips. When they finally parted, Gail couldn't stand still any longer. She rushed to Sam and gave her the biggest bear hug she had ever had. When Gail released her and turned to hug Jim, Sam asked, "Did I say yes? I was thinking it, but did I actually say yes?"

"Phil put his arms around her shoulders and with a firm hug said, "Yes you did, you actually said yes, congratulations to both of you. The two of you will be very happy and good for each other. You two stand here with the Parthenon behind you." Phil pulled the camera from his pocket. "We can't let this moment escape."

He snapped off about six quick shots. Phil was shaking Jim's hand when Gail cut in. "We're drawing a lot of attention here; I think it would be prudent to move on further away from the entry point."

"Good thought said Jim, "I noticed some people taking pictures with us in the zone." They moved on to the center of the Acropolis where the traffic was constantly moving. Sam's hand was firmly in the grasp of Gail. She was paying more attention to the ring than the monuments around them that dated back to the fifth century BC. The two were enjoying the moment to say the least.

"Jim my friend, you've just made life tougher for me; but I'm glad. You see, I have been wrestling with this decision too. It's a matter of when I know."

"No time like the present my man," said Jim.

"I wouldn't do that even if I had planned it for today, because today is your day. Besides Gail would think it was monkey see monkey do."

"I see your point, and appreciate it, just don't wait too long, she is a great person and loves you dearly."

"You're right, and I do love her." Phil asked, "How did we get fortunate to meet these two?" "Terrorism, I believe." Jim said.

Phil raised his eyebrows and said, "Damn strange world we live in my friend." The two men joined the ladies and continued their stroll around the Acropolis.

Time passed quickly. Soon it was time to head for the U.S. Embassy and their meeting with Timekeeper.

Reaching the Mercedes, Phil stopped short of unlocking the car. "We may not want to give the good news to Timekeeper just yet. We can't be sure how he will react." They all agreed to hold the announcement until after the meeting.

Traveling back toward the embassy was a short jaunt. Phil knew Athens and the surrounding area well. He turned the Mercedes north on to Dorileou, and where the side entrance to the US Embassy was located. Arriving at the gate, they were met by Marines dressed in battle gear and holding long handled inspection mirrors. While two Marines conducted a sweep of the undercarriage of the car, another was checking IDs. He checked his list and matched all names on it with the IDs. As he handed the cards back to Phil he said, "Open the trunk and hood please sir. We just want to make sure no one attached anything to you while the vehicle was out of your sight. "Good, thanks," Phil said. "In the trunk we have…," "I know what's in there sir, those items are authorized for you." He smiled at them, "You look clean, have a good day all of you." With that, the second gate opened for them to enter the compound. Phil proceeded to a spot designated for visitor parking. Figuring this was the end of the mission, and where they would turn in all the issued items, they gathered all of the issued gear, and proceeded to the working entrance.

# CHAPTER 38

**AS THEY APPROACHED THE** embassy entrance, the door opened as if it was automatic however, it was actually activated by another Marine guard stationed just inside the door.

"Welcome," he said. "Each of you please sign in the space provided beside your printed name, and please no discussions of classified nature until you are safely in your briefing area." They each signed in and waited for further instructions.

There was a civilian standing by, waiting for the sign in procedure to be completed. Jim was the last one to sign. As he finished, the guard checked the sheet carefully, looked up and said, "All clear, have a nice day, they are all yours sir."

The civilian waiting motioned them to follow him down a hallway to a large heavy door which he opened. As they entered the room they noticed a familiar decor. They took seats at a large wooden table similar to the one in Gaeta. Gail sat first, then Phil, Sam and Jim. The door closed behind their civilian escort who followed them into the room.

"OK, we can all be real now," he said. "Keeping quiet is tough at best, but when greeting visitors it is really tough because I want to welcome you but not get you talking and possibly say something outside of a sealed room that may aid our enemies or compromise any ongoing missions by the way good job on getting Masawi. Sorry about the run-on sentences but I just had to get it all out. My name is Greg."

"Wow Greg, that was impressive, all in one breath," said Gail.

"Didn't want you to think I was antisocial." They all chuckled and relaxed a little. "There are ears all around us. Every embassy and official foreign office has listening devices pointed at us, we only talk freely in rooms like this."

Phil asked, "What is the basis of this meeting, do you know?"

"I'll let your contact fill you in on everything." He smiled, "He'll be in momentarily, had to touch base with the Ambassador first."

Timekeeper entered the room from a separate door opposite the one they entered. "Great job last night guys. It's amazing how well things go when we don't over-think and plan and get too complex. You just went and got the job done. I suppose you all are wondering what this meeting is about, yes." The four of them all were answering with affirmative answers.

"The first thing is to let you know Mohamed Masawi is in the care of the CIA in Gaeta. He is no longer a guest of the US Navy. Did you recover Masawi's weapon?"

Phil reached in the bag of tricks and placed the Lugar Parabellum on the table along with four loaded magazines and thirty rounds of loose ammunition. "It was in the trunk of his car," said Phil.

"Good thinking to recover this weapon, it will never be used to kill another American. We will run traces on it, and see if it will connect him with anyone else, maybe someone who provided it to him."

"It looks like a collector's piece," Jim said.

"Yes, it is known as the 'Lugar Artillery'. I have one very much like it in my collection. Now for the main reason you are here."

They each readjusted themselves in the chairs, anticipating what was to come next.

"Each of you performed beyond normal expectations, I must start by saying that. I am here to request each of you stay on with the team, in the current roll you are presently filling. You have come together as a very effective operating unit in such a short time, and I might add, with such a wide range of abilities."

"As each one of you is aware, terrorism is on the rise in the Middle East and Europe in general and the world as well. As we approach mid-year 1984, already we have noticed an increase in terrorist activities over the previous four years.

I have been assigned to create a new Middle East terrorism tracking unit, and have cart blanch orders to do what it takes to get it up and operational within the next forty days. This unit must be small, tight knit, and unobtrusive. This would be much like your past assignment, but with a bit more risk to each of you in some ways, but less in others. We will take the next four weeks to train up for what would be expected of you as a tracking team. If anyone of you wish not to participate, it is fully understandable. I will simply look elsewhere, and get you back to your old jobs, but I feel confident in your abilities as a team, and I'd prefer to keep you all together.

Take a day or two to think about it, but I need to move forward with my plan within forty eight hours."

He turned to exit the room when Gail asked him, "Are we allowed to ask questions now?" He stopped and turned back to her, "Somehow I knew, and trusted, you would ask the first question," he said smiling at her. "I mean that in a positive way. Out of the four, you have the least experience in this type of work; but you are eager to learn and ask questions, I like that in a person. You can keep everyone focused and on their toes."

Phil, Sam and Jim chuckled amongst themselves. "It sounds like they agree with me."

She turned to them and said, "Thanks for the support, TEAM."

Timekeeper grinned at her and asked, "What's your question Agent Cornell?" She froze in place for a second, taken aback by his use of the term Agent.

"Agent?" she asked. He responded, "Is that you question?" "No sir, my question is, what about our active duty status? How will this be addressed? What will our status be?"

Timekeeper answered, "That will depend on you. I can offer you, any of you, a wide range of options. We can talk about that after you let me know, as a team, what your decision, or decisions, is or are." He turned to walk out of the room again, when Gail looked to the other three, "Well don't force me to make this decision on my own, you all know I'm in for the duration."

Timekeeper stopped again and turned, "So say you all?" Phil, Sam and Jim looked at each other and nodded in agreement.

Phil asked, "When does the training start?" Timekeeper smiled and said, tomorrow morning, 0800 this room."

He looked at Samantha and asked, "Have you set a date yet?"

She wrinkled her brow quizzically. "I spotted that rock on your finger before I came into the room. Remember there are certain people who would kill for that, so use caution.

Don't forget to refresh your bag of tricks; you will be keeping all that gear for now."

"No date yet," said Jim. "Will there be a problem with our personal situation?"

"Not if I'm invited to the event, whenever it gets scheduled." He turned and exited the room this time, and the door closed securely behind him.

Phil challenged Gail, "What have you done to us?"

She turned to him with a look of astonishment on her face. "What have I done? No one else was asking questions.

At that moment Jim, Sam and Phil broke into laughter. Sam said, while trying to stop snickering, "While your back was turned to us, and you were quizzing Timekeeper, we all gave him the thumbs-up; we were all in and waiting on you to commit; which we knew you eventually would do. You enjoy putting the bad guys away just like the rest of us, besides, what would we do without you?"

"My team and welcome to it," said Gail.

"But what did he mean by, Agent?"

Sam answered, "We're going to let you think about that for a while, it will sink in."

The newly formed team stood together. They were congratulated by Greg, their escort, who then returned them to the Marine guard, again without conversation. The Marine still on guard proceeded to sign them out of the building.

Again there wasn't a word spoken on the way out. As they exited the compound gate, the silence was maintained for a while until Samantha said jokingly to Jim, "Time for some Château de white grape?"

Gail injected, "I'll drink to that. Just the short transit from the conference room knowing you can't speak makes one thirsty."

Returning to the hotel, the conversation was limited, even though there was no restriction on communicating in the car. Each one of them again found themselves wondering what the future would bring, and how it would affect their relationships as a team.

# CHAPTER 39

**PULLING INTO THE HOTEL** parking lot, Phil suggested they have their celebration drink before going to their rooms. Sam said they should get a bottle of wine to celebrate in the room. Her reasoning was to allow them to speak more freely to each other and not worry about prying eyes and ears. Gail agreed and so they did just that.

Jim ordered appetizers from room service, along with two bottles of wine; one white, one red. The team gathered on the balcony of Jim and Sam's room and sat for some quiet discussion.

Jim asked Phil, "What do you think Timekeeper will offer us as career options?"

"I don't know for sure, but in the past I have known people that were placed on the retirement list for the military and signed on directly as company employees with benefits."

"So it was a smooth transition?" Jim asked. "Pretty much seamless," Phil answered.

"How would this work with Jim and me?" Sam asked.

"Almost the same, but you would have the option of returning to your parent agency for retirement if you wanted to later on," Phil said. "For Gail and myself, there is no going back to active duty; the decision is permanent once we leap. However we could remain on active duty temporarily assigned to Timekeeper, but without increase in pay or some of the benefits of being with the agency, but all the military benefits. As for me, I'll make the leap to the company."

"What about my situation?" Gail asked. "I have three years left to a twenty year retirement with the Navy."

"You will be put on the Naval Reserve list until eligible for retirement, you won't get shorted, may even get promoted to Senior Chief."

"That would be bizarre, getting promoted and never wearing the uniform." She said. Phil stated, "Yes, but think of the exciting things you get to do for your country, not allowed on active duty in the military."

"You have a strong point there dear, we can travel the world together and do good things that no one will ever hear of; but of course, isn't that the way of an Agent?"

Sam shouted, "By Gosh! I think she's got it!" Gail cut her eyes at Sam and said, "Stuff it Bitch." Sam responded, "Knock it off Blondie." They laughed and had a team hug, sat and finished the wine.

Tomorrow will begin a new life for them all, but for now they celebrated their future, and posed salutes to the fallen victims of Masawi.

Phil and Gail slipped off to their room and left Jim and Sam on the balcony.

"What do you think Sam?" "I think we will be a good team, but some day we will want to move on to our own adventures, probably no time soon, but the day will come."

He studied her face for a moment then said, "I think we, you and I, will be a good team no matter what." Sam moved closer to him, caressed the back of his head and drew him close for a long and eager kiss. Jim lifted her from the balcony and moved her gently to the bed. They undressed each other and as the two naked bodies met, they made love to one another unselfishly until, finally exhausted, the two fell into a deep sleep cradled in one another's arms.

## CHAPTER 40

**ARRIVING FOR TRAINING AT** quarter till eight, they went through the same silent sign in process only this time with a different Marine Guard. This time Greg met them with a large envelope under his arm. He smiled at them and said nothing. They followed him to the conference room that by this time had been converted into a classroom with two large tables with four chairs for the team to sit. There was a large screen television that doubled as a projection screen. Greg ushered them in then greeted each one by shaking their hands.

"Please have a seat and get comfortable, we'll get started by taking care of some administrative duties first. Have any of you decided overnight not to continue with us?" All answered negative to his first question. "Phil, you have been through this procedure before, did you explain any of the options to the others?"

"Yes, I covered the standard options."

"Good, the last time you chose to stay active duty, what say you this time?"

"I'm making the leap to full time." "Great." Greg said.

With that Greg pulled a smaller envelope from the large one

he had held under his arm. "These are your new credentials. Inside you will find an agency ID, passport and badge. Let me ask is there anyone who has chosen a different option?" Again the answer was in the negative.

"Wonderful, we can save some time." He handed out the remaining envelopes to the other three team mates. "They are individualized for each of you, we did some anticipation." As they all looked at each other holding their new credentials, the realization hit them that they were now all considered Agents of the CIA. Prior thoughts of their future paled as the thoughts of what they now held in their hands confronted them.

Greg broke the silence, "I'll take those visitor badges from you now. You all will use a different entrance and exit from now on." He smiled at them, "You can talk in the hallways on the other side, but never this side." He pointed to the door they just entered. "Take the next few minutes to check all the information on your new credentials, we're good, but typos do occur. We have coffee, water, juice and fruit in the rear of the room. You are invited to partake anytime you wish. Restrooms are through this door." He pointed to the door through which Timekeeper had been entering and exiting. They were now part of the real agency, not just part time help.

"Timekeeper will be in shortly to kick off your orientation and training sessions. We will have someone from personnel and admin come in to answer any of your questions concerning record transition, pay and other bennies." At this point Timekeeper came into the room.

"Greg, are we set?" "Yes sir, four new agents have reported for training." "Wonderful news Greg, thanks my friend. I've got it from here."

"Good to have you all on board, good luck," Greg said as he left the room.

"Well Agents, let me begin by saying how proud I am to have

you as a team, and how important this step is for the agency. You have an opportunity to write your names in the history of this agency. During the next few days/weeks, you will be exposed to much top-secret and above information. All of you have cleared the required background checks, and each of you are familiar with how to handle this info. We will cover tactics, covert activities, active investigations, major players around the world of terrorism, friend and foe, and law just to name a few, let's get started, any questions?"

Gail's hand went up, "Do you have a name?"

He looked at her, and answered, "Yes, Timekeeper, another question? Ok, here we go."

With that the training started. The next week was intense with all the new data coming at them, names, positions, affiliations with governments like Iran, Syria, Lebanon that are actively providing the terrorist with assistance in the form of equipment, money, training and safe havens; all part of the team's training. At the end of each day the team was exhausted mentally. Week two came and passed with the team stressed and exhausted to the almost extreme. The training was intense, more so than they had expected. At the end of each day they were so spent, mentally and physically, they traveled directly back to their hotel rooms, and went straight to bed and sleep.

At the end of week three, Timekeeper announced to the team that they would graduate early. Unbeknown to them, he had doubled up on some sessions, to allow them to finish ahead of schedule. Timekeeper recognized the teams' zeal for their mission, and pushed them just a little harder. They now realized this had been partly the explanation for the fatigue they felt at the end of each training day. Soon the team would be back in the operational field, and the pace would be more to their liking.

Sam asked, "Where do we go from here?"

Timekeeper smiled and said reassuringly, "You will not be

thrown into the fire just yet. As we discussed in training, we have many field agents imbedded with friendly locals. They keep us updated on day-to-day operations of the terrorist, not only as they move though the Mideast, but their intentions. We need to know more about the interworking of the various organizations associated with the Iranian and Syrian support system.

This is where you and your team will sniff around the edges and compile a report stating your findings. This report will be presented to the National Security Council. So you see your findings will play a part in the direction we will take this fight against terrorism."

The four of them smiled at each other with anticipation and concern. Each of them had their own mixed emotions concerning their individual fate, and the future in store for them as a team.

Timekeeper broke the silence, "You as a team have performed admirably, during not only the training sessions, but through your service with your former employers. We feel, and I in particular, have the utmost faith in your abilities to work together and produce results."

"Tomorrow you will have a day of relaxation and rest, make the most of it, you may not have much time for relaxation after tomorrow. I will contact you with your next assignment."

With that he turned and left the room through the door which they would use from now on when at this compound.

Again the ride back to the hotel was mostly quiet until Jim asked, "What in the hell have we gotten ourselves into?" The other three chuckled lightly. Gail said, "I was wondering if anyone else had that question on their mind."

Phil was driving the car as usual glanced at Gail and then into the rearview mirror. "I think that was probably on all of our minds."

Back at the hotel, Samantha said she thought that an evening of dining and dancing for the four of them was in keeping with their tradition. She felt this would be a great way to break some of the tension, and that it would be a welcome treat; sense the last three weeks hadn't allowed much time for activities like this.

They decided to dine at the hotel, and settled in for a delicious Greek fare consisting of, seafood, lamb and plenty of fresh vegetables and bread straight from the hearth. Any discussion about their future assignments was not mentioned. They sampled the red and white wines, and then finished off the evening with a cold shot of Ouzo. They headed for their respective rooms for a night of rest and possibly to indulge in another activity that also had eluded them for the training period as well.

Gail put her arms around Phil as they stood on the balcony. "I just want you to know, that no matter what comes our way, I love you."

He smiled lovingly at her, "We will be fine, our team is solid, and you know that I love you." In the adjacent room, a similar scenario was playing out. Samantha and Jim were feeling much the same as the two next door. The team, as a unit, was in synchronicity more than they could know.

# CHAPTER 41

**EIGHT AM A KNOCK** on the connecting door, it was Sam. Phil wrapped in his bathrobe answered. "Just a moment." He moved to the door, slowly opening it.

"You two love birds ready to see the sights?"

"Just out of the shower, we need about thirty minutes. We'll meet you for coffee in the dining room." Phil said.

"Sounds great, *old man*." Jim said from the bathroom.

Phil came back, "I've got your old man *Skippy*."

Phil smiled at Sam, "This is going to be an awesome group."

Sam said, "It already is, see you guys down stairs."

As Phil closed the door, he looked around to see Gail looking at him.

"You know, I really don't feel like going out and seeing too many sights today. My mind is still engaged in work, and what's next. I feel like moving on with it."

Phil smiled and said, "I know how you are feeling, and in some ways I am right there with you. But, we need to decompress a little to maintain our sharpness and let our bodies catch up. A little time away will do us all good."

Gail moved in closer and wrapped her arms around him. "I really don't care what we are doing, as long as you are there with me." Phil responded with a strong but loving embrace with her. He said, "We had better get moving before Sam and Jim come looking for us."

Phil and Gail entered the breakfast area that was set up in the dining room; they joined with Jim and Samantha who had once again ordered for the four of them.

Jim stated, "Hope you guys don't mind, I figured it may save us some time." Gail said, "That was very presumptuous of you, but of course you know that." She then looked at Jim with a grin from ear to ear.

"Then I presume you will sit down and enjoy your breakfast." Jim returned.

"Of course I will darling." Gail snickered back.

"I love this group of vagabonds," Jim said.

Phil chimed in with, "Too late now, Gail took care of that for all of us, we're stuck with each other." Gail landed a light punch to Phil's left shoulder.

"Wow", Jim said. "She hits like a girl."

Sam turned to him and said, "Watch it Romeo, I hit you like a girl and guarantee you will remember it." Jim suggested they eat breakfast before it gets cold and he gets bruised.

Samantha asked, "Does anyone else feel like a full day on the town is a waste of time?"

Phil and Gail both started smiling at each other. "We had this discussion prior to coming down from the room." Gail said. "Phil said we needed some decompression time, but it doesn't need to be all day."

As Jim and Sam looked at each other and nodded their heads, Jim said, "We had pretty much the same talk, we've been under the gun for three solid weeks preparing for whatever is in store for us, and it seems unnatural to take a day off now when we are so keyed up to get started."

Phil chuckled and said, "What do you say we go down to the beach for a walk and talk about it there?" That point was agreed upon, so after breakfast they headed for the beach.

Arriving at the beach, they removed their shoes, rolled up their trouser cuffs, and set off down the beach hand in hand. Many of the local inhabitants had arrived and staked out a spot to place blankets, lounge chairs and large beach umbrellas.

Phil and Jim noticed many of the women preferred not to wear tops, as clothing was optional at this beach. "Jim", said Phil. "Do you feel a little overdressed?"

"Not as much as Sam and Gail probably do."

After that comment Gail said, "We are a close group, but not that close. What are your thoughts on that Sam?"

"I think a little mystery is good for the imagination." She answered. "It keeps relationships healthy." The guys laughed and the four continued the stroll along the shore.

Lunch time came and found the team back where they had started. They had washed the sand from their feet and ankles and placed the socks and shoes back on their feet when Gail asked. "Anyone care for an American Burger?"

The other three froze for a moment and looked at each other. "I know I am not the only one that has been thinking about this for a while, but just what part does Georgiou play in all of this?"

"So you want to go back to the scene of the crime and poke around?" asked Jim.

"No poking, just eating, and possibly listening, and maybe observing."

"I thought you would never ask," Sam said. "That point has had me wondering too. He didn't sound any alarm that night, and

Timekeeper didn't mention him, so yeah, I would like to know a little more too."

Phil asked, "So I guess play time is over?" Gail pinched his cheek lightly, "If you're a good boy, its pie and ice cream for you tonight."

Jim looked at Sam with his eyebrows raised. "You can have desert too little boy, but you must be good the rest of the day." They snickered at their moment of childishness and headed off to the American Burger Restaurant.

"Well look who is working today," Sam said in a low but audible voice. "It's our friend Georgiou, what a stroke of luck."

Phil said they should set outside on the patio for observation purposes. Georgiou noticed them and started over to greet them.

"My American friends, welcome, please sit and enjoy. It has been a while since you have visited us." Jim reached out to shake his hand and Georgiou responded. "How have you been, well I hope."

Gail answered, "We have all been well, and you?" He responded with a big belly laugh, "I stay so busy cleaning tables; I sometime forget what I am to do next. Please, can I start you off with a glass of Agiorghitiko from Peloponnese? Much like the French Beaujolais only better, made with the St. George's grape. It goes well with anything on our menu."

Jim rushed to answer, "Georgiou that would be wonderful. We can decide what to eat and enjoy a taste of Greece all at once."

"Splendid, I will get your wine right away." With that he hurried away from the table and started preparing the wine.

Sam looked at Jim, "That was presumptuous."

"No," he said. "I have had this wine before and it is really good. I just wanted to share the experience with my family."

Gail was smiling, "Like that word presumptuous, do you?"

"Fits him to a tee," she said. "I've been waiting all day to use it on him just like you did at breakfast."

Jim was now grinning and shaking his head, "If you don't like it, I will drink it for you." Georgiou was now returning to the table with the four glasses of Agiorghitiko. "If you don't like this wine," Georgiou said, "it is on Mr. Jim." Everyone was now laughing, even Jim. They all sipped the wine and agreed it was delightful. "You are off the hook Mr. Jim," said the waiter. "I will give you a few moments to decide on food." "Thank you Georgiou," said Phil.

He turned and walked away.

Jim looked toward the other three, "That is scary, he remembered my name."

Phil said, "He probably knows all of our names and more. We'll have to pass this by Timekeeper tomorrow; just to see what he will tell us."

"Good thought, let's just have some fun now that we have incorporated work into our day. See what you've done Gail," Jim quipped.

Gail shot back, "Careful, I'll hit you like a girl."

For the next two hours they sat and enjoyed their conversation, food and of course Greek wine. Georgiou remained in the background, and did not interact with them any more than a normal waiter would.

# CHAPTER 42

**HAVING ARRIVED EARLY FOR** the meeting with Timekeeper, gave the team a chance to set and enjoy coffee and some Greek style pastry. They all took turns guessing where they would go next. The general opinion was Israel, but when and what city was a challenge. The question would be answered in just a few minutes.

Timekeeper entered the room. "How did you guys enjoy your day off yesterday? Was the Agiorghitiko to your liking?" He looked up at them and smiled.

Phil spoke first, "Gail was right, Georgiou is connected."

Timekeeper chuckled, "He is a Greek operative of the, Greek Special Operations Command. He has been assigned to us here in Athens to help gather Intel. We had a bet among us on how long after training it would take you guys to go sniff him out."

Gail asked, "Who won the bet?"

"Let's just say he owes me a bottle of the stuff you were drinking last night. It is supposed to be good; how did you like it?"

Sam spoke up, "They went through two bottles of it, and so it must have been good."

The other three started snarling and laughing at the same

time. Timekeeper held up his hand and laughed, "I think I have my answer."

"Let's get this briefing started. As you all are aware, Hezbollah had its seeds planted after the Iranian Revolution in 1979, although it wasn't known under that name until 1982. This revolution gave cause to the rise and melding of the government Iran with the Muslim religion. Yes they have a president, but the Aitolia calls the shots. This was done, as they say, in order to give representation to the oppressed and downtrodden in Iran, and surrounding Muslim countries.

Of course the United States was credited for all their problems along with Israel, whom they considered, to be an extension of U.S. policies. We know this was not entirely the case but, they had to blame someone, and they did want the USA out of the region."

"We are also aware that Iran is supporting this revolutionary Islamic movement in Lebanon since the latter part of 1982, by sending in forces from Iran to actively support the cause of Jihad, *Holy War* against Israel."

"This Shia group, keep in mind I'm speaking of the militant portion, in Lebanon is where Hezbollah originated. We have learned that the Shias in general represent a little more than forty percent of the population there, and have felt they have been under represented since Lebanon won its independence from France in 1943. One area is of particular interest to us at the moment is, and will be your next assignment; Beirut."

"Since the coordinated attack on the French peacekeepers and the U.S. Marine barracks in October last year, there has been rumblings of more of these suicide attacks being planned. Your job is to sniff out any information you can get your hands on concerning these planned attacks."

"You will do this while under the guise of being reporters for the Canadian National Press. You will leave tomorrow afternoon for Paris, France. There you will receive your Canadian passports and press credentials. I don't believe the language will be a problem. From there you will be flown in to Beirut along with a group of legitimate press agents from around the world. Any questions so far?" Everyone sat quietly and somewhat stunned.

Phil cleared his throat and asked, "Where will we meet our contact in Beirut?"

"Your contact will find you, probably as you check in at the hotel. All correspondents will stay together. Let me remind you, these are horrific and extremely dangerous times, but you know that."

"Be mindful of everyone you meet or make contact with. Rely on your instincts and training. In this case, one assumption is allowed; assume everyone wants something from you. Are there any more questions?"

Sam raised her hand and quickly withdrew it realizing she wasn't in school, "What is the timeframe we are working with to accomplish whatever it is we are to accomplish?"

Timekeeper smiled and said, "Look, I realize you were probably expecting to be sent to Israel, but this is where you are needed now, and all will fall into place for you as you get further information from your contact in Beirut. He has interviews set up for you with pre-determined questions. Things are almost scripted out for you. I have faith in you guys, your good at improvisation. I expect you to be there no more than two weeks, give or take."

The team sat and glanced back and forth at one another.

Greg entered the room and greeted everyone. Timekeeper continued, "Greg will collect the paraphernalia from your last assignment, and your contact will supply you with anything you need in Beirut. Happy hunting, and take some good Kodachrome pictures."

With that he left the room and as the door closed behind him, Gail sighed, "What have I gotten us into?"

Greg watched as they were all beginning to laugh at Gail's comment, and their new situation.

"Here are your airline tickets to Paris; you will be met by a Canadian representative there with further instructions. I wish you the best my friends." He turned to leave the room.

"Greg, what does Timekeeper mean when he said we will be in Beirut for about two weeks 'give or take'."

"Jim, I think it is usually about ten to twenty percent, give or take." With that Greg turned and left through the door.

They looked at each other again in amazement at Greg's answer.

"One o'clock flight to Paris," Phil chuckled. "This reminds me of my last experience years ago." The others looked on and waited for him to elaborate. "This is what happens when they get full confidence in you; or total lack of the same. As an operative you are expected to fill in many of the blanks. This should prove to be interesting."

"Beirut, what could possibly go wrong?" Sam said tongue-in-cheek.

"I need a glass of Chateau de red grape," announced Jim.

"I believe we're all with you on that one," said Phil.

Gail had moved to the back of the room where the Greek pastry layout was. "I think a couple of these bad boys are required just now too, 'a'." Sam quipped, "She's got the language thing under control."

Again the trip back to the hotel was mostly silent, with the exception of comments on the ridiculous traffic. Phil glanced into the rear view at Sam and Jim silently gazing out of the windows. Gail to his right was staring straight ahead not commenting on anything. Phil thought this was most unusual for her. "Penny for your thoughts," he said.

"Don't waste your money" she said. The remainder of the trip was silent.

# CHAPTER 43

**THE FLIGHT TO PARIS** went without a hitch. So far things were going as planned. After gathering their baggage and clearing customs, they were met by a rather young looking man with a Canadian flag on his lapel. He was holding a sign that read, Welcome Jim, Sam, Gail and Phil.

Phil noted, "Nothing like being obvious." The young man watched as they approached and lowered the sign.

"Hello, my name is Robert, welcome to Paris." Gail asked, "Robert, isn't that a little risky holding a sign with our names on it?"

"Not at all," he returned. "You appear to be tourist this way. It's when we get all cloak and dagger that everyone notices. Bring your bags now, we're off."

He led them to a waiting limo at the curb. The banner on the side had Parisian Tour Company on it. After all bags were loaded, the passengers took their seats. Robert drove around for a few minutes checking the rear view often.

Phil noticed this and asked, "Expecting Company?"

"Not really," Robert answered as he turned down a narrow unoccupied side street. About half way down the street he stopped the car and let the windows down. He reached out the window and retrieved the magnetic sign from the driver's side of the car.

He looked at Phil in the passenger's seat and said, "Do be a sport, and bring in the sign from your side please." Phil reached out and did as requested. "Now we can proceed to our next stop. Simple steps you know are the best in most cases. No one really watches the Canadian Embassy that closely yet, but I am sure that will change some day too."

Phil said, "Yes, I hope it isn't today."

At the embassy, they were led down a long hallway to a meeting room where there were several hard case bags stacked. Robert pointed to them and said, "These are your props. All the cameras and film you will need to look authentic. I will go over any of the equipment with you that you wish, but most of it is point and shoot. No weapons of any kind will accompany you on this leg of the trip. Be prepared to fly out at eleven am tomorrow, we have hotel rooms for you tonight."

Robert continued, "A standard taxi will take you to the hotel tonight and pick you up at nine am tomorrow morning, any questions for me?" They were all silent. "Good, you will be on your own until tomorrow morning. The taxi number will be 752546; the driver will be red-headed and female. If these items do not match, do not get in the vehicle. Enjoy." With that Robert disappeared.

Phil said, "I guess we gather up these boxes and head out the front door. If there is a taxi there with all the matching requirements we're set."

Dragging all the baggage with them, they left the front door of the embassy and through the security gate without as much as a nod from anyone.

"There is the taxi," Sam stated. "Red-headed female driver in cab number 752546; we're golden."

The driver was silent as she assisted in loading the baggage.

On the way to the hotel, the driver handed Jim a card with nothing but a phone number on it. "If anything changes, call this number and ask for Sally."

"OK, Sally," Jim said.

"Sally is not my name; Sally is just the person you ask for."

"Roger that," said Jim, as he smiled at her in the rear view. Nothing more was said the remainder of the way to the hotel. When the bags were unloaded, the driver simply drove away leaving them standing in front of the Parisian Hotel.

Gail said, "I guess we're where we are supposed to be; let's go inside and see if we have a reservation."

They approached the front desk. Gail spoke, "Reservation for four under Cornell."

Jim said, "Talk about presumptuous."

"The man behind the desk searched his ledger. "Ah-oui, two rooms on the third floor."

Gail looked at Jim and said, "I am the finance manager for the group you know."

At the doors to their rooms they stopped and made plans for dinner, agreeing to meet back in the lobby in thirty minutes. All went well that evening and morning was soon upon them. Dragging all their baggage behind, they met for breakfast.

"Zero eight hundred and we are ready to go," Sam announced. "I hope things go as well on our next stop. Did anyone else notice how almost cold the people were at the Canadian Embassy, it was like no one wanted to have much to do with us."

Phil said, "Yeah, it's called plausible deniability; they are willing to help, just not get involved to deeply. If anything goes wrong, they can still deny any involvement. You notice we were not required to sign in and out of the embassy. That means no paper trail. Our passports would show up as stolen if anything happens."

Jim ventured, "So you're saying we're pretty much hung out to dry if we screw this up?" Phil chuckled, "Give the man a kewpie doll."

Gail mused, "This crap just keeps getting more bizarre every day."

Phil laughed, "Welcome to the world of covert ops."

Gail said, "I used to wonder how all this covert stuff worked. Now I'm in the middle of it, and I still wonder."

Phil said, "It works because of people like us and Timekeeper, Greg, Georgiou and even Roger and Sally or whatever her name is."

"I guess you have a valid point," said Gail. "Just what is a Kodachrome anyway?"

Sam said, "Oh my dear God, this is going to get interesting."

Zero nine hundred and the taxi pulled to the front of the hotel precisely on time. Each of them checked that the driver was correct the cab number was correct; so they loaded the bags in the car.

"Good morning Sally!" Jim shouted. The driver jus glared at him in the rear view, then finally a faint smile. No conversations on the way to the airport. As the bags were being unloaded, the driver looked to Jim and said, "Good luck to all of you." Before anyone could say thank you, she was gone.

"Jim," said Gail, "If I didn't know better, I'd think she was flirting with you."

He said, "Yes quite the conversationalist isn't she." He turned to Samantha, she looked him dead in the eyes and pointed two fingers at her eyes and then toward him, giving him the universal, I'm watching you, signal. Phil and Gail were pulling the bags and trying hard not to laugh.

Check in went smoothly as this was a chartered flight sponsored by the international news agency. Once on board, they settled in and waited for takeoff. Time passed as they winged their way toward Beirut.

There was excitement in the air from the correspondents

with the international press, but there didn't seem to be much apprehension among them. Some of the same correspondents had covered the barracks bombing the previous year, where 241 American military personnel were killed in the largest non-nuclear explosion on the planet since WWII.

Clearly terrorism was on the rise not only in the Middle-East, but around the European Continent as well.

The roar of the jet engines changed pitch. By the sound and feel of the aircraft changing its normal attitude, passengers knew they were about to prepare for landing in Beirut, Lebanon.

Phil had been napping and was awakened when the aircraft changed its speed.

A stewardess came around and handed a scarf to all the women on board that were not wearing one and asked them to place it on their heads, as was the custom and requirement of Muslim countries.

The aircraft was on final approach to the airport. Gail was looking out the window at the green and brown mixture of the mountainsides. As the airplane came closer and closer to the runway, she could see signs of war; burnt out vehicles, buildings with only two walls standing, pock marks and craters in the streets, a multitude of holes in walls and buildings that were still standing, all caused by continuous small arms, mortar and rocket fire.

She turned to Phil and said, "Just think, this place was once referred to as, 'The Paris of The Orient'. What a crap-hole now. I guess if they were unhappy before, they are ecstatic with their progress now. Backwards doesn't even come close to describing this sight. But the ones that suffer are the everyday average people that just want to raise a family and be normal."

Phil said, "Makes you wonder about their tolerance, right? Most Americans really do not know just how good we have it."

# CHAPTER 44

**AS THE TEAM DEPLANED** down the portable stairway onto the tarmac, they commented on how they each were feeling a new kind of vulnerability to the open elements.

Blue hatted United Nations Troops were standing along their walkway with machine guns at the ready. The passengers all hastened to get to the cover of the small terminal where they were being directed. Here they had to clear Lebanese customs.

Now officially in the country as Canadian press associates; they were taken to the hotel that had been designated for all arriving press members. When checking in at the hotel, they were separated with women in one room and the men in another.

"These folks take this separation of non-married people seriously don't they?" Gail posed.

Phil smiled, "We will set up one of the rooms as an office to work from, and there we can spend most of our time together. But our mission is always first, we will have to keep that in mind especially while here."

"I understand that completely, it's just the fact we weren't given a choice or even asked."

Phil smiled again and said, "Wait until you forget to wear the hijab, and a stranger reminds you in a threatening manner to cover your head. You will not be allowed in public without it you know."

"Whatever," Gail said. "Let's get on with this job and get back to civilization as soon as possible."

Samantha had listened to all of this and inserted, "I guess it's you and me girl. We'll have to help each other through this trauma, as long as it takes."

"I can't think of anyone better to suffer this degradation and indignation with, besides scarfs were the rage in the fifties back home, it'll be 'Deja vu all over again'."

Jim said, "I will still see the two of you in the same way as before, my very trusted back-up and I am yours as well. We are still a team; with no chateau d' grape of any color shape or fashion."

"Your right about that Jim," Gail said. "This will probably be tougher on you."

Realizing the moment, all of them had a good laugh, and resigned themselves to focusing on the task at hand.

They were escorted to the separate rooms on the fifth floor, with the women on one side of the hallway and the men on the other. The office had to be set up in Jim and Phil's room, as it would have been improper for the men to enter the woman's room, but the women were allowed to enter the official office room to work. After unpacking and arranging the audio and photographic equipment in the office, a knock came on the door.

Phil moved to open it. There stood a man about five ten, black hair, with a backpack slung over his shoulder.

"Hello I'm Eric Moore, your contact here. May I come in?"

Phil said, "Sure if you have some proof of ID." Eric looked up and down the hallway, reached in his shirt pocket and produced his Canadian passport. Phil looked at it carefully. "Come in Eric, this is Samantha, Gail and Jim." They exchanged greetings and handshakes.

"How was your trip in?" Eric asked.

"Wasn't a bad flight, all went well," Phil answered.

"Good deal," Eric said as he busily opened his backpack. He produced four Walther PPK 380 pistols. "These will be your last line of defense, you are not to produce them unless you know you are about to die. Anywhere you go you will be escorted by UN Peacekeepers, but if you're ever out on your own, well, you're on your own. Not recommended, but it happens time to time; any questions? Not yet anyway I guess. Here is a map of the area. On it there is an emergency egress location, memorize it. This is where you go if you have to use your pistols. This is for absolute emergency egress. An inflatable boat will be there to whisk you out of here, and to a ship patrolling the coast."

Sam asked, "Just what the hell are we supposed to be doing here?"

Eric looked at her and answered, "We have a contact within Hezbollah that you will interview. We cannot contact him directly, but his organization has cleared him to be interviewed by a foreign news group other than a U.S. press. He will during this interview hand over information concerning future strike plans for the Islamic Jihad movement, and organizational plans. It is of the utmost importance this information gets back to your contact Timekeeper, not me. You may or may not see me again. This is why I'm covering all this so quickly.

When you leave tomorrow with the press group, you will be put into a vehicle with just the four of you. You will be selected by two blue hats with UN patches, they will call you Quebec. As the column moves forward they will be redirected to a meeting point where you will meet Amid Hyzone; the supposed mastermind of the barrack bombing. Some say he had a change of heart after the bombing and wants to get out of the business, some say it's a false front to protect the real perpetrator. Before that happens he supposedly has some information he is willing to give up for our help in his disappearance."

"You mean we will be helping a man that killed all those people?" asked Jim.

"First of all, we don't think he was the mastermind, we believe it was Subhi Tufayli. Hyzone was credited with it originally by the Iranian government; he claims to us that he had nothing to do with it, but is playing along with the Iranian claim until we can get him spirited out of the country. He believes he was set up to take the fall for it, and become the hunted one while taking the heat off of Subhi Tufayli; the real mastermind behind the bombing, and we do have proof of this. We don't know for sure how long he will last before his own people kill him; blame us and thus making him a martyr."

"So we get in there tomorrow, interview him, somehow he sneaks us some information, we bring it back for evaluation, then he gets spirited away," Gail stated.

"Yes, you've pretty much got it!" said Eric.

Sam said, "What could possibly go wrong with this plan?"

Eric said, "Great, then you're ready to go. Don't forget, Quebec, tomorrow; best of luck!" With that he let himself out, and disappeared down the hallway.

The four of them now stood quietly puzzling over what had just occurred. Phil looked up at the three stunned team mates and asked, "Anyone want to go home?"

All three raised their hands. Although they knew at this point going home was not an option, they felt obliged to answer the question honestly, and by this time Phil's hand was in the air as well.

Jim finally broke the silence, "I guess we need to plan our question and answer period."

Phil held out a sheet of paper with questions to be asked already lain out. "It was in the map case."

# CHAPTER 45

**THE FOLLOWING MORNING THEY** met for a quick breakfast. "How did you girls sleep last night?" asked Jim.

"Not good, the shelling over in the Beqaa Valley kept us awake most of the night," said Sam.

"Us too," said Jim. "Look at the real news people, there all excited about this, hard to believe. We probably stand out by not acting all atwitter about this crap."

"Well we'll be out of here soon, and excited in our own right," said Phil. "Everyone just do your job today, and we'll be ok."

"I'm glad you're so optimistic," said Sam. "I'm just use to better planning."

Phil said, "In this business, this is a good plan. But I know what you mean, I feel the same way; we will pull this off."

The time came to load up. There was much clatter and confusion amongst all the press folks. As the four walked out dragging the cameras and such, they heard someone shout, "Quebec, over here." They all turned, looking to the left. There stood a six foot well developed man in his early thirties. He motioned them over to the vehicle.

He assisted them in loading the equipment into the two and one half ton six-by transport truck, affectionately known as, *a duce and a half*. The truck had a Browning fifty caliber machine gun mounted in a turret ring on the passenger's side. Other than that, the four blue hats were carrying US made M-16 rifles. Phil noticed two additional M-60 machine guns, loaded on the floor of the truck. He also noticed one of the blue hats also carried an M-79 grenade launcher.

"These guys are loaded for bear," he commented to the team.

"That makes me feel better," said Gail. "Here I am with a pea shooter."

Sam stated, "Let's not forget to leave our *pea shooters* in the truck when we go in for the interview."

"Yeah, to forget that, could be fatal," said Phil.

The caravan pulled away from the hotel, one following the other. Taking up the rear the team was busy looking through the small slits in the armor shielding that was surrounding the outside of the vehicle. Although the plating did not give total protection, it did provide a higher level than nothing at all.

After about a mile the vehicle suddenly turned left, leaving the safety of the rest of the column. Soon they were on a secondary road headed in the direction of Jeita Grotto, about twenty kilometers from central Beirut. Things were looking more countryside than city, but still not like home.

The driver slowed the truck and turned onto an unpaved road. The ride became a little rougher but soon the truck came to a stop. The young man that had initially called them over to the truck at the hotel, now stood at the back of the truck.

"This is as far as we are allowed to go. You have about one hundred yards to cover on foot." The guards stood watchful as the team unloaded the gear.

"Here, put this on," said the leader of the blue hats. He held out a wrist watch. "It has an emergency signal built into it, just push this button three times and the Calvary will arrive. If you have to use it stay on the ground because anything standing will be killed, promise. Leave any weapons here, they will frisk you. If you don't come out within forty-five minutes, we will come in. Good luck."

"Thanks, nice to know you are on our side," Sam said.

"More than you know Ma'am." The team started the short football field length hike down the dirt road.

Two scruffy looking men slowly moved out of the brush. They were holding AK-47 rifles across their chests and didn't appear friendly. The men waited for the foursome to reach them, then motioned them to raise their hands for searching. One man did the searching while the other kept an eye on the others. He seemed fixated on the women more so than the men.

Following the thorough search, they were motioned to follow further down the road. Standing at the end of the dirt road was an adobe type shack with wooden plank doors and cloth shutters covering the windows. Clearly this wasn't a stronghold, only a meeting place for very short meetings.

The two guards motioned them inside. Entering the hut, they noticed three armed guards standing, and a single individual seated at a small wooden table.

He stood up and spoke, "Welcome, come in. We must get started; I only have a short time."

Gail and Sam removed the cameras from the cases and placed them on their shoulders ready to film. One guard stepped forward and motioned with his hand across the lens, no!

Amid quickly interrupted, indicating it was authorized. "Pictures of me only, nothing more."

Phil asked the first question: "Are you the mastermind of the attack on the Marine barracks?"

The answer came quickly, "No, I am to be used by those in

power, Sheikh Subhi Tufayli is responsible, and I am a scape goat for the Iranians."

Jim was standing by with a note pad, putting it all down in writing, plus anything else he observed. Phil asks the next question: "Why do the Iranians want to use you this way?"

"They think my people are sub-human, we are Sunni Muslim. We are used when it is convenient for them not to get their hands dirty."

Phil looked around the room, "Are these men Sunni too, and are they loyal to you or Tehran?"

"The men with me are my brothers, but more of my brothers are being held against their will until I return that is why I cannot leave now, they are suspicious but have no proof. This movie will provide proof for them, and is why we need to move for approval quickly. When this is shown to the world, I am a dead man along with my brothers, so you see I am serious."

"Why don't you save yourself and these brothers with you now?" Jim asked.

"On top of the hill behind us are rockets and mortars and machine guns pointed at us now, I know this. They believe I am claiming all the glory for the bombings in this interview. After this confession is shown to the world, I would be killed and made a martyr for no reason, and my brothers killed also, this I know."

Jim looked at Phil then asked the next question: "We were supposed to get something else."

"You will find it in your camera case; it was placed there during your search. Now we must be done, our time is finished. Please ask your people to move with haste, our lives are at risk each hour that passes."

"Thank you for your time and courageousness in coming forward, we will do everything we can to expedite this." Phil said.

"May your God watch over each of you." With that, Amid

turned and walked out the back of the house. No one said a word until the gear was packed up and they were back on the dirt road out with their escorts. Phil turned to see if the guards were still watching, but they were all gone.

He said, "That wasn't at all what I was expecting."

"Not at all," said Sam, "not at all."

As they approached the truck they noticed it had been turned around and pointed outbound. "Welcome back, everything go as planned?" asked the young blue hat.

"Better than expected, say where are you from anyway," asked Phil.

"North Carolina," he answered. "How long you been with the teams?"

The man smiled at him and said, "You must be navy, ten years," he answered.

Phil smiled and started putting the gear in the back of the truck. "I do like your blue hat disguise," Phil said. The young man answered, "Effective."

On the trip back to the hotel Gail started thinking out loud. "Maybe this means we can get out of this hellhole earlier than expected."

"I hope you're right," Jim said. "I could sure use a Chateau' de Grape."

This brought a chuckle from the other three along with agreements and a somewhat lighter mood. They still had to get these results back to Timekeeper.

Sam mused, "I don't believe the boss was expecting what happened today. I think he believed that Amid would put on a strong front claim responsibility; and then slip us the info some other way."

"Speaking of that is the info in the bag?" asked Phil.

"Sure is," Gail assured. About the time she answered, there was a loud, *tink*. "What was that?" she asked.

One of the escorts said, "30 cal., probably a local hoping to score a lucky hit from a distance, happens all the time." She snuggled up closer to Phil and sat quietly for the rest of the ride.

## CHAPTER 46

**WHILE UNPACKING THE GEAR** back at the hotel, Jim said, "Wonder if we will hear from our friend Eric again anytime soon?" Gail responded, "You mean Mr. I've got all the answers. That guy just doesn't sit right with me."

Phil risking being accused of taking sides said, "That's the nature…." Gail broke in, "of the business. I accept that, there is just something I can't put my finger on with him. I don't mind a hat, but this damnable scarf has to go."

"You are in one hell of a mood girl, what's up?" asked Sam.

"You're right, that goon taking his time and feeling me up this morning didn't set right with me for one thing, he took longer on me than you is another, and the way the other one was looking at me gave me the creeps."

"They knew you didn't like it, so they took pleasure in that. I winked at him when he started with me and it scared him off. Don't worry about it; if we don't succeed in what we're doing he'll probably be dead by the end of the week."

"My God Sam, you really know how to make a girl feel better." "No, just how much better we have it, than him."

Gail thought for a moment then said, "You've made a good point..., thanks. I'm still wondering about Eric though."

"Anyone hungry?" asked Jim. "I'm going down stairs and see what I can scare up."

"A nice Delmonico would be nice," Phil said.

"I may have to go kill the cow myself," Jim shot back.

"Make it a clean kill; otherwise you may toughen up the meal." Gail said.

Everyone stopped and looked up at her. "What?" she said. "I had an uncle that raised Angus beef cattle, that was his favorite saying."

Shaking his head and laughing, Jim gave Sam a kiss and went downstairs.

He had been gone about five minutes when there was a loud explosion and the building began shaking. When everyone regained their composure, Sam screamed out, "JIM!" and took off out the door in search of her fiancée.

Phil realized they had violated a cardinal rule, never go anywhere alone. By now all three of them were standing in the hotel lobby watching Jim running across the street to another hotel that had just been car bombed.

"Phil, go get him, he doesn't see danger even when it's looking him in the face." Jim knew he was in one piece, and his instinct was to run toward the danger and help those he could. Phil caught-up to him and snapped him back to reality.

"Jim! Jim! Let the experts handle this; you're placing the team in jeopardy. The media is taking pictures of all of this; let's get out of the way!"

Jim glared at Phil and then softened his expression, and shook his head in agreement. Together they withdrew to the safety of their hotel. Sam couldn't help herself.

She ran to Jim and embraced him with tears of joy streaming down her face.

"God, I thought you were gone. We've got to get out of here." They rushed back up the stairs to the office room, where they all held on to one another tightly. Moving closer to the, now cracked window, they looked down on the carnage.

"What madness this is," Gail stated. "Harmless innocent people killed and maimed for no good reason."

Phil held her tightly. About thirty minutes later they realized what little power they had was now gone. Now literally on their own, they barricaded the door, charged their pistols, and settled in for a long night.

"We've got to get a little sleep," Phil stated. "Jim, you and Sam get some rest; we'll wake you up in about four hours, and trade shifts."

With that Sam and Jim moved into the bedroom to try and sleep. "This has been one hellacious day," said Phil. "I'll be glad to get out of here too. This is no place for a lady."

Gail smiled at him and said, "A lady's place is with her man, where ever that may be, even this hellhole."

About midnight there is a soft knock at the door. Phil grabbed his pistol and eased to the door. "What do you want," he asked.

"It's Eric, open the door." Phil and Gail started moving the barricade far away enough from the door to allow him to peek out and verify that it was Eric and he was alone.

Everything seemed clear, so they opened the door to let him in. Eric stepped in and closed the door behind him.

"Where are the other two?"

"Sleeping," said Gail.

"Wake them up, get all your gear together, were getting you guys to the embassy annex." "What is going on?" asked Phil.

"Get your shit together quickly; I'll answer your questions on the way."

Gail went to wake the other two and was greeted by two drawn Walther PPK's pointing at her. "Damn guys it's just me." They lowered the weapons. "What's up?" asked Jim. "I'll tell you like it was told to me, 'get your shit together, were moving to the embassy annex', Eric is outside. I knew I liked that guy."

They packed hurriedly making sure to take everything. Moving everything out, they hurried down the stairwell and exited through the rear of the building.

With most people still focusing on the calamity out front, no one noticed their exodus. There was a Range Rover waiting for them. The driver was someone he recognized from earlier that day. Phil pushed Gail in the seat and slid in behind her.

"You look different without your blue hat," Phil said. The driver smiled in the rearview and said, "I have to get work where I can find it, mouths to feed you know."

"I understand," Phil said.

Once loaded they took off slowly and quietly moved through the streets of midnight Beirut. A few minutes later they arrives at the embassy annex gate.

The driver shut off his headlights and turned on his right hand blinker. This was a pre-arranged signal to open the damn gate, I'm in a hurry and I'm coming in one way or the other. The guard on the gate was one of the escorts they had earlier also, so everything was cool. The gate shut behind them.

"Breathe a little easier now folks, we're a little safer here."

Phil said, "I think we all need a little sleep."

Eric said, "We'll take care of that after we review your interview from what is now yesterday. I'm sure you know time is of the essences."

Jim said, "Yeah, we were informed of that, so let's get on with it. From the sounds of it these guys need a decision fast."

Eric asked, "What all did Amid tell you?"

"Everything, things you guys were probably guessing at," stated Jim. "I think it is hotter than you believe, the interview was straight forward and to the point. He did slip us a disk with more information on it."

"Great," said Eric. "Let's start with the interview tape."

Eric sat there listening and watching Amid's responses. "Well I'll be damn," said Eric. We expected him to claim responsibility for the bombing and then slip us some vital info via some other means, but this is hot stuff. Things must be tightening up around his camp."

"Sounds like that is the case," said Phil. "He said if he didn't return back to the camp all hell would rain down on us and he and his brothers would be killed."

"What's on the disk?" Eric asked.

"Don't know; we had no way to read the disk, and not to mention, there was the small problem with the hotel across the street from us."

"Let's plug it in and see what is there."

After spinning up and loading a document unfolded. "Damn," Eric expressed.

"It is a list of all planned attacks in the Middle East, and Europe. We've got to get this on the company wire ASAP. You guys rock, your boss was right. He said all I had to do was point you in the right direction and stay out of your way."

"He said that, did he?" Gail asked.

"Well yes, or words to that effect. We're working on getting you out of here tomorrow. But now I know you need sleep."

Gail said, "My opinion of you keeps going up." Phil's face turned red, while Jim and Sam were giggling like school kids.

Eric looked them, "Yep, you guys need sleep."

213

## CHAPTER 47

**EARLY THE NEXT MORNING** Eric rousted the four from slumber. "Revile, revile, got to get moving you guys! You can sleep on the plane." Slowly they grumbled, stretched, scratched and moaned.

"Do we have time for a shower?" Gail asked.

"Very short and quick one," Eric said. "We're running out of time and water."

"There goes the opinion poll again," she said.

"Eric you've got to get consistent if you want to maintain a high rating."

"I'm more interested in keeping you alive. We found out the embassy annex is on the target list." With that, everyone started moving a little faster.

Phil asked, "When do we get out of here?"

Eric said, "There is a C-130 leaving out of here in ninety minutes and you guys are scheduled to be on it."

"What do we do with all this gear we brought with us?" Jim asked.

"Leave it here; it's all agency equipment anyway, and it'll help get you out of here quicker. We have to clear you through customs with your Canadian passports to keep things manageable for our friends to the north. If you feel the need, do a quick splash-and-dash in the sink. When you get back to Athens, you can slow down and readjust from there."

"Eric, you seem to be agitated more than just by trying to get us out of here; what is going on?" Phil asked.

Eric looked at him sighed and then started to explain, "That bomb yesterday was meant for you guys. Two days ago, the press was scheduled to stay across the street from where you ended up. Your reservations were changed yesterday morning due to plumbing problems at the hotel you were scheduled for; the one that was blown up. The bomber didn't get the change notice. Chatter has it, there on the way here next. That is why I'm sweating bullets trying to get all of you out of here. It may make it safer for everyone; especially us"

"Thanks for the honesty; I'll put the squeeze on the others to be as efficient as possible."

The few bags that were being taken with them were hastily thrown into the back of the Range Rover. "Hustle-up, we don't have time to waste." Phil urged. Everyone piled into the vehicle and was barely in when the driver started rolling forward.

Sam searched Jims face for an answer to what was happening. He just shrugged his shoulders. Gail turned to check on Jim and Sam. She wrinkled her brow in a way as to silently say 'what the hell'?

Phil adjusted his position as to face the other three. "Sorry about the rushing, but Eric said that we were the target of the bomber yesterday, and chatter has it that the annex was next. So you can see why they are in a serious rush to get us out of here."

Gail said, "So these radicals are after us?" Phil was silent, his head moved up and down indicating an affirmative answer.

Out of nowhere a white pickup truck was now on their tail. The escort car in the rear started firing at the truck. As they rounded a curve to the right, two rounds of small arms fire struck the bullet resistant window beside Gail. Her reflexes were quick; she covered up and ducked down as did they all. The rear escort scored several direct hits on the pick-up. The truck rolled sideways spilling the passengers in the bed onto the street and then rolling over them. The two gunners in the rear escort vehicle gave each other the thumbs-up. The three vehicle convoy continued on to the airport. Eric was in the lead vehicle and radioed back to see if anyone was hit.

The Range Rover driver picked up the mic and answered. "Dirty shorts, but everyone is fine!"

"Roger that!" came the response. "The entrance is just ahead, we'll be inside the compound in a minute or so," the driver announced.

After clearing the entrance manned by U.S. Marines, they drove toward the small building where they had first cleared customs coming in to Beirut.

Eric jumped out and ran to the team. "Got a little excitement on your way home," he shouted. "This is far as I go; you are on your own again. The Air Force will take care of you now." He handed Phil a small sack. "This is a copy of your interview and disk. We made copies just for you guys. All of this was sent to Timekeeper via courier overnight, while you were sleeping. Thanks for everything, good luck."

With that he turned and climbed back into his vehicle. Each of them grabbed their bags and thanked the escorts for getting them to the airport safely. Like something out of a Wild West movie, the escort vehicles spun around and headed for the gate.

"I've got a bone to pick with Timekeeper," said Gail. Phil laughed and said, "It won't do you any good." "No, but It'll sure make me feel better."

Jim and Sam were entering the shack arm-in-arm. Gail reached out to Phil and slid her arms around him. "I'm glad we were together when all this happened, you give me the strength to endure this crap."

Phil held her tightly, "I am glad we were together too. Now let's get the hell out of this shooting gallery."

Their Canadian passports were stamped for exit, and the Air Force Police Sergeant escorted them to the waiting C-130. The engines were spinning up waiting for them to board the aircraft up the loading ramp and get buckled into the strap seats. Soon the airplane was powering up and making a quick turn out over the Mediterranean Sea in route to Greece. Each of them breathed a sigh of relief while snuggling in closer to their chosen mate. The loud droning of the four engines soon faded into sleep.

# CHAPTER 48

**AFTER THE C-130 HAD** touched down in Athens, everything went as is often said in America, like, "a piece of cake". Jim, Sam, Gail and Phil, woke up in the U.S. Embassy to soft music and clean surroundings. Gail asked Phil, "Have we transcended into heaven?" Phil grinned at her, and said, "Absolutely yes!"

Samantha and Jim were just beginning to wake, when the phone rang. Jim rolled over and reached for the phone.

"Yes," he answered, listening for a moment he said, "Yes, we'll be there, thanks."

"What was that?" Sam asked. "Timekeeper, he wants us to be in the briefing room in thirty minutes. Let Phil and Gail know will you, I've got to go the head."

Gathering in the briefing room, Gail led the way to the back of the room where all of the goodies were spread out on the table. "I thought we had seen the last of these wonderful delights," she said.

Timekeeper entered the room. Everyone looked around at him, "Please help yourselves, I'm a little early and you have been through a lot in the last day or two. We have time to settle in a little before we get started, no rush." He started setting up his presentation slides while the team was refueling in the rear of the room.

Timekeeper joined them in filling a plate of fruit and Greek pastries. "This stuff is defiantly habit forming," he said.

Gail glared at him for a moment then said, "Yes, it's deadly." He kept filling his plate and said, "Point taken." He smiled at her and returned to the front of the room.

"Please have a seat, and bring your food with you,"

Timekeeper announced.

"The Embassy annex in Beirut was bombed last night and at least twenty people were killed. I'm sending you four back to the states for further training and preparation; besides that, it think you need a break from this for a while. You will be kept up to date on all the continuing events in this region, and in many cases you will be more advanced that the ones of us remaining here."

"Again I am so impressed with the way you all have handled every situation that has confronted you. You have each performed superbly and without a doubt beyond expectations. However, we owe it to you to see you get the best training and information available if you are to continue in this agency. Your success has allowed me to continue the pursuit and formation of terrorist tracking teams in the Middle East."

"We owe it to you to provide you with the best the U.S. has to offer. This is why I am choosing you four to return stateside to help advance this mission. In the future we are convinced terrorism will play a dominant role in foreign policy and in everyday life worldwide. We feel the need to expand all aspects of counter terrorism and intelligence in this area. Our country must take the lead on this, because it is in our best interest for future generations to come. Does anyone have anything for me?"

Jim asked, "Any word on Eric?"

"I'm afraid he may be among the missing at this time," answered

Timekeeper. "We'll get you out of here tomorrow to London. You'll stay there the night and fly out the following day to Washington. Agency representatives will meet you there and give you any assistance you may need from there. You will be allowed to take some time off if you want." He looked at Jim and Sam. "Take care of what business you need to during that time. Your schedule will be demanding after that." He smiled at them then said, "However don't rush into anything."

Jim and Sam understood his meaning.

"You guys have much in store for your future, enjoy the now, and take time to appreciate each other. You all have much to offer in the way of service to humanity, ahead of you. Prepare yourselves well. I am proud to say I serve with you."

With that he turned and disappeared from the room.

Phil turned to Gail and said, "I think he was trying to avoid your wrath by leaving so abruptly."

"No," she said, "I think he is reluctant to see us go."

Jim confirmed, "I think you're right, but he knows we will be back, only stronger and more prepared. The world and terrorism will continue to move forward. The United States is, and has always been, the target for anyone with a lost cause; we're a soft touch you know. These people have nothing to live for but attract attention and international money to their cause. They do not respect life or any form of life unless it is on their terms. They called it Islam, but is it? I don't think so, not in its purest form."

"All I know for sure is, brother; my priority at this moment is to plan a wedding," Jim looked at Phil and grinned, "or maybe two?"

# THE END

(To be continued?)

# MY SPECIAL THANKS

I would be remiss in my duties if I did not thank the one very special person whom encouraged and soothed my 'ill temper' throughout the writing and editing of this book. My wife Vicky, for more than 49 years has been my building block and guiding light; I cannot thank her enough. My sister-in-law Vicki Walker; thanks for her editing and encouragement.